The Business
of Baker Street:

Five New
Sherlock Holmes
Cases

William P. DeFeo

Paperback ISBN 978-1-80424-602-3
ePub ISBN 978-1-80424-603-0
PDF ISBN 978-1-80424-604-7

Published by MX Publishing
335 Princess Park Manor, Royal Drive,
London, N11 3GX
www.mxpublishing.co.uk

Cover design by Awan

Table of Contents

This book is dedicated to the members
of my paternal, maternal, nuclear, and marital families,
many of whom appear in these pages.

The Case of the Harried Clerk

My breakfast had not been very satisfactory. It was part of the new regimen my wife had imposed upon my slowly expanding waistline. She said that a doctor should be an example of good health to his patients and then continued to argue gently the proposition that eating toast without butter and jam was a beneficial ujndertaking.

"Rubbish," I replied mildly, and returned to the columns of the *Times*.

The morning edition had its usual offerings of indictments, assaults and burglaries, all of which invariably turned my thoughts to my former roommate, the celebrated London detective, Mr. Sherlock Holmes. It had been some time since I had heard any news of my friend, although it always seemed to me that between the lines of certain newspaper crime reports the powerful influence of Holmes's deductive methods shown through. Some two or three of the stories had what I recognized as his indelible stamp. My reading of a succession of these was sufficient to persuade me that too much time had passed since I had paid Holmes a visit. I resolved that very day to turn my steps in the direction of the detective's current and my former lodgings at Baker Street.

I descended from the carriage, crossed the road, stepping up on the curb in front of the familiar dwelling. I ascended the stairs as I had so many times, with the old faint feelings of adventure swelling up slightly just under the rib cage. I entered the room unannounced as always and was surprised to find it quite empty. Having had a slow office calendar the entire week and more time than I would need to run the few errands that had been carefully ordered by my wife, I determined to wait the better part of an hour against the possibility of Holmes's return.

It was not an altogether uncomfortably cool afternoon in early April, and though the fire had not been lit, I settled myself in the large armchair by the fender and took up a copy of a monograph that Holmes was apparently preparing. The posting address appeared on the blue card stock cover: "The London College Forensic Review." It was one of the science journals that regularly published Holmes's varied research. The article was of moderate length dealing it seemed with the classification of the visible characteristics of various punctures of indigenous insects. I had hardly scanned the title when there came the footfalls of at least two persons upon the stairs. I assumed it was Holmes accompanied by someone, until I heard a very tentative knock at the door.

Considering my friend's absence I was quite uncertain how to respond, but I finally rose and opened the door to find the young boy in Mrs. Hudson's employ, and a short, heavyset, middle-aged gentleman standing rather sheepishly behind him.

"Mr. Fowler for Mr. Holmes," the boy announced without surprise, being accustomed to seeing me with some regularity on the answering side of the door to Holmes's apartment.

"I'm... afraid... Mr. Holmes is not in," I replied stammering, rather taken back by the awkwardness of my circumstances. I had no reason whatsoever to be caught short by being alone in the detective's rooms, and yet I was uncomfortable. It struck me curiously that more often than not, even in the most honest of circumstances, an honest man cannot help but be tinged by an uncomfortable feeling of guilt. I recovered from my musing quickly and squared myself formally to the visitor.

"How do you do Mr. Fowler. I am Dr. Watson, Mr. Holmes's associate."

The man pulled the watch from his waistcoat pocket, raised the spectacles from his nose to read it and stood by in a manner clearly indicating his nervous agitation. Finally, after an uncomfortably long hesitation that included the careful adjustment and re-adjustment of his spectacles, he communicated that if it were not an inconvenience, he would very much prefer to wait for Mr. Holmes's return. When he saw my hesitation, he assured me hurriedly that other engagements would almost certainly prevent his waiting much past a quarter of an hour.

I ushered him into the room with what courtesy I could muster, and he sat down upon the divan. When he politely ignored my attempts at pleasantry, and it became clear that he would keep his counsel, I recovered the monograph and made show of devoting myself to the reading of it. I was certain the man had not arranged a meeting with Holmes in advance but had simply made his appearance at Baker Street in hopes of finding the detective at home. My certainty in this was beyond question. Holmes would never have knowingly absented himself from an appointment. Personally, he was a mass of disorder and unpredictability, but professionally his habits were inflexibly regular. The notion of a missed appointment was, I knew from long experience, anathema to the exacting nature and strict propriety ingrained in the man.

At first the visitor was at his ease, although formal, indeed almost severe, in his deportment. As the minutes passed, however, his presence of mind flagged, and his agitation slowly began to make itself known by his niggling on the divan and by the nervous attentions he paid to repositioning his spectacles.

I knew Holmes well enough to be certain that if he did not return in time to speak to this overanxious guest, the detective would question me closely regarding all the details of the visitor so that he might, as was his fashion, draw conclusions as to the gentleman's person, position, and circumstances. I therefore immediately turned my attention to the fellow and began a thorough, yet discreet examination of the man and his accoutrements.

He was of less than moderate height, almost perfectly rotund, with a very closely shaven face, and deep-set brown eyes behind small oval spectacles. His clothing proclaimed him a man of business I was certain; despite his obesity he was well-tailored in jacket and waistcoat, with striped, grey pants, well-turned soft leather boots and gray striped gaiters. His very white shirt, starched collar, and carefully handed cravat completed the picture of a fastidious, if not fashionable, London merchant, or perhaps a solicitor for an office of advocates down Old Bailey way.

Considering Holmes's absence, I was determined to gather the very minutia of details as grist for my friend's deductive mill, but search as I might, aside from the observations noted, the visitor was to me as uniformly conventional as a London streetlamp.

When fifteen minutes had passed, the fellow rose and with a hurried bow left the room before I could halfway accompany him to the door.

It was not ten minutes later that Holmes slowly entered the room, glanced at me casually and without any further greeting, flung himself down into the armchair with a listless smile. I had known him too long not to have noticed the signs. A drudging *ennui* had set itself upon him like an equatorial fever. These bouts afflicted him with regularity. Not a fortnight would pass after having applied his mind to the solution of some knotty intrigue than he would succumb to a lethargy that transformed him to his core. His friendly words could not disguise the languor of his subdued condition.

"I am glad to see you Watson," he said tiredly, "though I fear that your visit has come at a time doubly disappointing for you. You are an hour and a quarter past your old housekeeper's excellent luncheon, and in the bargain, I am without at present a matter of interest upon which to engage your assistance. I am afraid, my old friend, that present circumstances make me an unworthy host."

"Well, I have had an early lunch," I said agreeably. And as for your prospects, they may have just improved. There was a gentleman here to see you not 10 minutes ago."

"That is well," he continued without conviction, "but I have little faith in it being a matter anything but conventional. You will remember from your own experiences that conventionality in crime is the rule. You chronicle only the exceptions, dear doctor. For every "Case of The Speckled Band," for every "Boscombe Valley Mystery," there are legions of conventional crimes – committed without plan, solved without thought, and brought to law with as little effort as it takes to lift a quill and write the word 'conventional.' Just by the sheer weight of probability, the gentleman you speak of brings us a conventional matter. But let us not despair entirely," he said with some little determination in his voice. He roused himself in the chair and reached for his clay pipe and pouch of shag.

"Tell me of him and of his story."

"I am afraid there is no story to tell. He came to see you, waited some little time and left. But as I knew you would inquire of me, I made a point of examining the fellow in every possible detail. If you wish I will communicate to you every particular so that you will have the man complete."

"Pray, proceed," he said earnestly as he thumbed tobacco into the blackened clay. I began with as much specification as I could bring to bear, starting as I thought best with the gentleman's hat, with a thought to work my way down his person in an anatomically organized fashion from top to bottom, a method second nature to me by my years of medical training. I was just about to move rather proudly to a refined delineation the visitor's mien, when that same tentative knock at the door I had heard earlier came again, and upon my pulling open the door, the same urchin announced again, "Mr. Fowler to see Mr. Holmes."

Holmes put aside his tobacco and crossed the room in an instant. He took his visitor's hat and ushered him genially into a chair near the hearth. In deference to Holmes's mood, I thought it best to open the dialogue myself. I turned to our guest and asked him how it was that he had cleared the "other engagements" he had told me of, and how he knew that Holmes had returned.

"In truth," he said with some small embarrassment, "I had no other engagements, doctor. I apologize for that small deceit, but I am so put upon by this troubled business I seem to be losing my usual civil habits. Forgive me. When I left your rooms, I lounged at the corner of Baker and Sutherland wondering what I should do. When I saw a gentleman on the flags, a tall gentleman of a serious disposition, and he turned up the steps of 221B, I knew it must be Mr. Holmes."

"I commend you on your observation," said Holmes, "but tell us please the nature of your business here. And speak frankly, if you will. Dr. Watson's ears are a second in trust and faith to my own."

"It is a tale whose burden I have carried for the better part of two months. I will begin with myself by way of introduction. My name is Charles Fowler and I…"

"You may proceed directly to details other than those made obvious by your person," said Holmes demurely. "Namely, that you are Charles Albert Fowler, that you are a clerk in the British Maritime Bank and Trust Company, that you are 43 years of age, unmarried, a Freemason, and that you are at present deeply disappointed with your barber."

Fowler's mouth dropped open as stupidly as a coal chute, his eyes went wide, and his arms rose slowly up as though to ward off a blow. "How could you…you couldn't possibly…," he stammered in disbelief.

"My dear sir, I have merely done what you have done in your observation of me as I arrived home, though I have drawn conclusions from what I observed. The small service pin on your lapel is marked 'BMBTC.' It is wrought in silver to represent twenty-five years of service, and I perceive it is quite new as it is utterly untarnished. Common knowledge informs that British banks employ clerks not sooner and seldom later than their eighteenth birthdays. The indent on your right index finger is from years of grasping the stylus, and the slight shine and thread wear on the lower, right-hand sleeve of your coat denotes the perennial labors of the clerk. Your bowler, that lies there upon the sideboard, contains your full name, next to which appears a faded though still recognizable emboss of the square and compass. And the residue on your hat brim of Linden's No. 3 Professional Darkening Hair Pomade, are signs that you still hope to secure the interest of some member of the fairer sex. The smudge of Linden's on your handkerchief proves that your barber was inexpert in his recent application of the paint. But pray continue with your tale and leave no detail untold."

Fowler collected himself slowly as he came to realize that the facts Holmes had gathered were not sensational, but rather deductive and drawn from sources of information that were there for any eye to see. As plain and rational as it was, once its rudiments were revealed, Holmes' penetrating method of observation and conclusion was nonetheless an utter fascination to both myself and Fowler. Finally composed, the gentleman took up again the thread of his narrative.

"The trouble was slow in coming, Mr. Holmes. It began on the second Thursday of last month, the day the bank's salary envelopes are handed out by the bursar. I was sitting at my desk in the corner of the office where I share space with the desk of the senior clerk, John Camberley. Between us we prepare all the ledger entries for all the trust disbursements for the BMB&T.

"Well, I opened my envelope and counted my money quickly, as the office was not fond of employees frittering away company time on personal enterprise. From between the pound notes there slipped onto my desktop a small plain white card. As you may imagine, Mr. Holmes, the bank is very regular in its habits and a card inserted into a salary envelope was very irregular indeed. Before I could think very much upon the irregularity of the thing, I read the characters childishly scrawled on the card face.

"Here is a reasonable facsimile of the card," he said, and handed Holmes a plain white card showing the following entries:

> '*GBSTF*
> *(d) 150 pounds - 3Q'*
> '*Give thought to Nan!'*

Holmes scanned the duplicated writing summarily, then looked back at the clerk. "Would you be so kind, Mr. Fowler, as to propound upon your understanding of these entries."

"It is very clear, Mr. Holmes, or I should say it would be very clear to any familiar with the shorthand coding of the trust division of the BMB&T. The words on the card are in the nature of an order to create an expense of 150 pounds for the third quarter of this year as against the GBSTF, which is the Greater British Stevedores Trust Fund. I can only assume the words, 'Give thought to Nan' was a reference to John Camberley's afflicted sister, a very sweet young woman, though cruelly and undeservedly disturbed in the mind. You should know that the Stevedores trust is not my account, Mr. Holmes, it's John Camberley's.

Mine is a very cautious – a very exacting occupation Mr. Holmes, and I had no mind to speculate on the note's intent, but it certainly appeared to me that it was calling for the felonious entry of a fabricated payment."

"If you will permit the interruption of a few questions, Mr. Fowler," Holmes asked calmly. "For one, how are you sure it was 'fabricated,' and not a *bona fide* request in the ordinary course of business?

"Pardon me, Mr. Holmes, but as you concluded, I am a clerk these five and twenty years. Orders to disburse against a fund balance are never submitted by scribbled note sir. They are ordered in triplicate, signed each by the trust branch administrator, and accompanied by sheaves upon sheaves of paper that stand in proof of the actual expended monies. No sir, this note was surely a circus side-show business all round.

"Very well, yet if you thought so," rejoined Holmes, "why did you not alert the force at a local station house?"

"As for the police...." Fowler explained with a hesitation that bespoke the raising of a subject upon which he felt deep conviction, "if it is at all possible, Mr. Holmes, I should like to avoid any public discredit that may light upon the company. Ringing an alarm would do the firm a harm it does not deserve. It may be true that I am neither manager nor shareholder, yet the BMB&T has been good to me and my family. I am a bachelor as you divined, Mr. Holmes. My aging parents rely even more than myself upon the good fortune of my employment, if you see what I mean sir."

"I do, my good man. And how did you then proceed….be particular!"

"Well, sir, I turned with the card in my hand and said, 'What do you make of this, Jack?' and handed him the note. It seemed to take a moment or two for the weight of the message to hit the mark, but when it did, his eyes bulged; he turned as white as cod's flesh and mumbled that the card was meant for him and that he would attend to it. He slid it into his waistcoat pocket and sat the rest of the day as restless and fidgeting as a man tied to a stove top. But as he was a fellow not much given to either good health or good nature, I thought little of it further.

"What you have told us thus far Mr. Fowler might well be a succession of events conveniently explained by any number of fortuitous circumstances."

"That is certain, Mr. Holmes, and I thought it so myself until the occurrence of two further details. Here is the first."

The clerk handed my friend an evening edition of the London Sentinel turned to the lower left portion of the fourth page. A single column gave just ten lines of print to the death of "….a clerk of the BMB&T, one J. Camberley." The two inches of tintype went on to say that the body had been pulled from the Thames just north of Baywaters Bridge at Leighton, and that considering the absence of any evidence of malice, it was anticipated that the inquest would return a finding of accidental death.

"And now, sir, for the second. I arrived at work Monday last to discover that I had been ascended quite unexpectedly to the senior clerk's position. I moved my trappings into Jack's desk with, I might add, no small feeling of regret for his unfortunate end. But life's designed to go on, Mr. Holmes, and so there's an end of it, or so I thought. Three days later, the second Thursday of the month had come round again, and I was looking forward to my pay envelope with earnings at the new position rate, when this fell out with the pound notes."

He handed Holmes a plain white card written on one side in what gave appearance of little more than a childish scribble. It read:

"LCMET,
(d) 200 pounds, 4Q.
Give thought to your parents,
and to Camberley. "

Holmes leaned forward in his seat and faced the clerk squarely. He placed the card carefully upon the lamp stand beside him. With elbows on the chair arms, he slowly brought together the fingertips of his hands before him. "This is a dark business," he murmured. "May I venture a supposition that the LCMET is the bank's shorthand for the London City Museum Endowment Trust?"

"That is correct, Mr. Holmes."

"And might I also suppose that you now harbor a growing fear that you must choose one of two equally disagreeable paths, namely, to become a felon by committing financial malfeasance and face ruin and disgrace, or disregard the note and perhaps share a fate similar to the late John Camberley?"

The clerk blanched whiter than his shirtfront. He could neither respond nor contain any longer the unsettled emotion he had for several weeks struggled to keep within. He lowered his face into the palms of his hands, his frame shook in spasms, and muffled groans issued from a heart overborne with a long-controlled anguish. As a seasoned veteran of the healer's craft I have seen my share of human suffering, yet it is still unsettling to the eye and the ear when a man, expected too often to bravely endure the "thousand shocks," is finally overcome by them and surrenders to despair as Fowler did.

To his credit, the clerk indulged his sorrow but for a moment. He took hold of the short crystal of brandy that Holmes had poured and offered him and quaffed it gratefully. His color returned, and regaining his lost composure, he lifted his eyes to Holmes and said in a hoarse voice, "What's to be done, then, Mr. Holmes...., what is ever to be done?"

"Permit me but a few more inquiries," the detective said mildly, "and after your replies are made you may place the entire burden of the matter upon me."

"I will presume that your branch administrator is not the party responsible for calculating the contents, preparing, and distributing your wage envelopes?"

"No, Mr. Holmes, he is not," the clerk murmured in a voice not fully recovered from its disturbed passion. Those functions are performed exclusively by the office of the bursar. However, wage envelopes do pass through several offices and hands before actual physical delivery is accomplished. I see the direction of your thought but determining where the introduction of the card might have been made along its journey seems quite impossible. And I cannot imagine anyone in the employ of the BMB&T who would ever conceive of such a plan as this, Mr. Holmes. It is abominable!

"And finally, when must you complete the financial postings for trust accounts so as to be prepared for the fourth quarter of the fiscal year?"

"Not for a fortnight yet, but each day that passes brings me closer to a desperation that is like to be the end of me, Mr. Holmes."

Holmes placed a steadying hand upon the clerk's shoulder as he handed him his bowler, and after the customary exchange of thanks and reassurances, Fowler departed, though for all that, nonetheless agitated than upon his arrival.

Holmes sank deeper into his armchair and resumed his tobacco, but with no jot of the lethargy that had plagued him only half an hour earlier.

"This is a matter both dark and delicate," he said, "and it is far from the conventionality of which we spoke earlier. And did you hear him, Watson? He could not imagine, not by any stretch of his reason how anyone of his fellows could conceive of such a black plan of extortion. How fortunate are those as he...to have so trusting and so innocent a nature in regard to our species. You and I, Watson, are not so fortunate as that. In our little 'adventures' we have seen too close the features of the beast more times perhaps than men should have to see."

It was not uncommon for my companion to wax philosophic regarding the dimensions of his occupation, but I knew the musing would be short-lived in light of the intrigue that called now for the active application of his mind.

I was correct in this, for hardly a moment passed before he had sprung from the chair with a vault, taken up his heavy desk glass and began searching the surface of the card minutely, holding it to the lamp light, placing it to his nose, feeling the composition of the stock, every fiber of every sense focused on the small, white rectangle. This meticulous survey carried through the better part of half an hour before Holmes turned from the task with an expression that my long acquaintance with the man quickly discerned as satisfaction. To be precise, it was hardly an expression at all, but more a subtle settling of the physiognomy, not unlike the effects of a strong stimulant administered to one who teeters on the verge of losing consciousness.

"Extortion is a crime heavily laden with cruelty, Watson. The perpetrator derives no small delight in the secret, inexorable manipulation of his victim. Of course, the end purpose is not unlike that of most crimes, namely the monetary enrichment of the criminal, but riches are not enough to satisfy the cruel nature of the extortionist. There is a demonic aspect to extortion. Crime for mere gain can be understood, even forgiven by circumstance, but extortion is first and last a beastly business."

"But Holmes," I rejoined, "if the manipulation is secretive as you have said, how can a plot of extortion ever come to light?"

"Such plots seldom do. They bind their victims so tightly that few escape, save for the final liberation of the grave. You recall the matter of 'The Boscombe Valley Mystery,' Watson. It is true that that plot unraveled, but the victim never again knew peace of mind."

"Then I must repeat the entreaty of the clerk and ask you, 'what's to be done?'"

"We are fortunate in this one exigent, Watson – that our much-troubled Mr. Fowler has broken the chain of secrecy by placing the secret into our hands. And it is an obligation that we must undertake without delay."

Holmes scuttled into his dressing room with his customary deliberation and in a few moments returned transformed. His aspect was unaltered but his dress, from top to toe, was exchanged for that of a drearily composed London businessman. With a pair of crooked spectacles, a battered leather briefcase, and a worn topcoat that declared the extent of proud English economy, Holmes joined the legions of the city's "men of business." He crossed to his bookshelves, withdrew the year's copy of "Dickson's London Mercantile," and proceeded to transcribe onto some foolscap, certain listings from the volume.

"Could I impose upon you Watson, to man the home station until my return? I am off to do some shopping, and with a little luck, I should return with a guest."

*   *   *

The better part of three hours had passed before Holmes reappeared. His look was subdued, but the vigor of a new case and the call to action had completely transformed him. The sour depression that had gripped him only hours earlier was so completely gone that it would hardly be believed that the man of the morning and the man of the evening were one and the same. His business weeds seemed awkward to him now and he went to his room without ceremony and re-emerged shortly as Holmes. He sat heavily at his desk, pushed aside his monograph and looked once again at the card that Fowler had given him.

"I have been to five stationary shops in and about the neighboring streets of the BMB&T – five. The first four returned nothing, but the fifth 'paid the freight.' It has always been a curiosity of mine, Watson," he mused, "that the determined search we make for a particular datum seems never to yield a positive result on the first or second attempt. It is as though the sought-for result is veiled from us and we must trudge and stumble through shadows before gaining the reward. Five stationers, my friend – why do you suppose we never strike the vein on the first or second?"

"I am sure I do not know, but really Holmes," I replied with some irritation, "tell me what you discovered."

"It is not very much – hardly enough to satisfy the effort. It seems the card stock note that appeared in Mr. Fowler's pay envelope was purchased from Shipman's Stationers in Leggard Road, West End, and the parcel of cards was sent by post to the offices of the BMB&T."

"Then surely the payment can be traced by store records to an exact purchaser," I rejoined with enthusiasm.

"That is the sticker, Watson. The order for the cards was but a small part of the regular stationary order. It was placed and payment accomplished through ordinary channels of the BMB&T account that has stood with Shipman's for many years. We have pursued the rabbit only to lose it in a tangle of briars."

"And what of the' guest' you hoped to produce?"

"I fear that is yet another briar patch, my friend. Mr. Savins, the bursar of the BMB&T, is the epitome of an English man of business; very formal, very cautious, and for all but matters of business, very aloof. I barely gained entrance to his offices, even in my guise as a fellow member of the business tribe. Finally, I was forced to acknowledge my disguise and disclosed who I was *de facto*. When I explained that I was making discreet inquiries into the death of John Camberley, Savins recoiled, almost violently, and unless my evaluation of human speech has missed its mark, there was a palpable fear in his voice."

"What other signs of *mens rea* can you possibly need, my dear Holmes. Surely the man is involved or knows more of the matter than he is letting on."

"You may be quite correct, Watson. However, you may also be neglecting to give proper weight to the strong loyalties and noble allegiance of the dedicated British merchant. Such protective fidelity to their commercial obligations is the mark of many a good English businessman.

Savins may be an extortionist and murderer, or he may be a selfless and dedicated employee. On occasion, we need to cast our net beyond the obvious. It occurred to me that removing the extortionist from the comfort and security of a professional setting might allow the breadth of his darkened character to reveal itself. I have asked Savins to join us here for a simple dinner. He agreed, but did so with a reluctance that belied strong misgivings."

"Misgivings," I exclaimed! "Holmes, clearly you are describing the motions of a man possessing a guilty mind. If he breaks the engagement or fails to appear, it is certain he is involved in Camberley's demise."

Although I offered this declaration with all possible conviction, Holmes remained quietly unmoved. It was characteristic of his nature to hold rigorously to his own notions. However, unlike so many other passionately self-possessed persons, he did this without antagonism or presumption. It was simply a matter of his unshaken trust in his keen observations and implacable deductions. His silence after my pronouncement of suspicion regarding the bursar was characteristic of my friend. The silence was broken by a ring of the bell at the street, the pad of feet upon the stairs, and a knock upon the door.

Holmes moved swiftly to the door, opened it, and with his usual geniality he ushered the visitor into the room. He did not seem in the least surprised that the guest was not the BMB&T bursar, Mr. Savins, but a rather plainly dressed, middle-aged woman.

"Good evening, Miss Keel," Holmes said warmly as he steered her to the divan. "It was so good of you to come. Permit me to present my associate, Dr. Watson," at which introduction I smiled weakly, muttered her name by way of greeting and resumed my seat.

"Do I correctly presume," continued Holmes, "that your supervisor was unavoidably detained and has sent you as his envoy?"

Miss Keel sat bolt upright and took little notice of her surroundings as women are wont to do when they enter a room from obligation rather than personal design. She kept her eyes turned towards my friend, but never directly. She was one of those persons who made a habit of slightly averting her eyes from her conversant. Whenever her glance was drawn to Holmes' she would look quickly down or to the side, or slightly up over the detective's head. It was a disagreeable trait and did much to detract from her otherwise moderately handsome features. She was accoutered in the drab, colorless style common to women working in the world of the London office. This included a simply cut gray dress that fell modestly to the floor and ran high about the neck. All decorations to her sex were very noticeably absent, and her general deportment matched her wardrobe perfectly. Whether to her credit or to her loss, she was in voice and figure and manner, a mere business machine.

"Mr. Savins is a very busy man," she said in a temperate and efficient staccato. "The British Maritime Bank and Trust is his highest priority. The bank's reputation is sacred to him. In deference to his position and in his employer's best interests, he has instructed me to tell you that there is nothing further he can contribute to your investigation."

The content of this blunt declaration made by the bursar's secretary turned all reasonable suspicion, I was sure, to the bursar. It was certain Savins was the culprit. When Miss Keel concluded, I tried my utmost to catch the attention of Holmes and exchange a knowing glance, but before I could, there came a heavy knock on the door.

Without rising, and all the time smiling most intently at Miss Keel, Holmes said, "Come in Inspector – the door is open."

With three distinctly military strides, Inspector Lestrade of Scotland Yard gained the center of the room. He removed his hat, and in a respectful gesture to the lady, made a slight and clumsy bow.

"Allow me to introduce Inspector Lestrade. Inspector – Miss Keel of the BMB&T," said Holmes demurely. "I would offer you a seat, Inspector, but we are almost finished here and you should not be detained for more than a few moments. Have you sworn out the warrant of arrest?"

"Yes, Mr. Holmes. It's all in order, sir, and signed by the magistrate," Lestrade declared as he removed a folded blue legal back from his coat pocket.

"Excellent," said Holmes. "And am I correct that under present English law, any person of lawful age who is not a party to a legal proceeding may serve a warrant upon another?"

"Yes, once again, sir, though it's often a nasty business in the criminal cases."

Holmes took the warrant and reviewed it casually. "I do not foresee any 'nasty business' in the service of this particular criminal warrant, Inspector." He turned to face the secretary and handed her the folded papers. "Miss Keel, would you be so kind as to make service of this warrant on Mr. Savins tomorrow morning?"

"Warrant? A warrant for what?" she exclaimed incredulously.

"It is a warrant for the custodial arrest of Geoffrey Helm Savins under charges of extortion and complicity in the death of John Camberley," said Holmes with perfect composure. It was soon apparent that the cool austerity of the woman sitting on the divan was not a mere pretense. Her posture remained erect, her face was an implacable mask, and when she finally spoke, her voice was sure and steady. She rose slowly from her seat, straightened herself to her full height, and turned to the detective.

"No....no," she said decisively. That will be quite impossible, Mr. Holmes."

"And why is that" the detective asked in a voice that had hardened considerably. For the first time she turned her eyes full upon my friend.

"Because Mr. Savins is a family man with wife and children, and for those reasons he is a considerate man and one of high moral character, and additionally..., because he is innocent of the charges."

She rose from her seat and crossed the few paces between them until she was very close to where Holmes stood. Her demeanor had little changed from its rigid control, but a shade of color had come to her face. She stood before him, and it almost seemed from her stance that she was restraining herself from striking the detective. When her voice came to her, it was hardened and had the righteousness and arrogance of a woman deeply wronged.

"Bachelors," she said, slowly pronouncing every syllable of the word with a snarling vindictive anger. "They disgust me. They should every one of them be punished for what they do to my sex. Primping their independence about with their superior airs, while the women in their circles pine their lives away with waiting and dreaming and hopeless empty plans. Camberley was such a man, and Fowler too. I hated them. They left me to wither, year after year, until my youth was gone, and what beauty I possessed was gone, and my dreams of children were gone." Her face twisted itself into a grotesque smile. "So, I wrote them little notes. Little 'love notes' on little cards. I knew the prospect of committing extortion under the threat of harm to loved ones would torment them – I wanted to torment them as I had been tormented. And I watched it all...from my desk – watched them wither day after day and turn pale and despair. How can I describe it," she said dreamily with her teeth showing through the cruel smile. "Yes, ah yes, it was exquisite."

Lestrade stepped forward, gently placed his hand on her arm, and turned the secretary quietly out of the room.

The arrest warrant had fallen from the hand of the distracted woman as she left and I retrieved it. It was a blue cover folded over several blank pages of legal bond.

"Then you knew that Savins was innocent," I asked as Holmes fell back into his chair and casually reached for the draft of his monograph.

"I knew," Holmes replied, "only what the evidence provided. The note card was a treasure of information. It declared the existence of an insider at the BMB&T. The handwriting on the card was barely legible. This indicated that the victims knew the regular handwriting of the extortionist. My terse discussions with the bursar resulted in one important fact; Mr. Savins' handwriting appeared on virtually no documents in the clerks' offices. Miss Keel prepared all documents for Camberley and Fowler." When, after considerable effort, I was finally able to make clear the details of the matter to Lestrade, he agreed to the innocent charade of an arrest warrant."

Holmes fired a match and lit his pipe with the familiar disinterest creeping into his voice and manner.

"Also," he continued languidly, "a cursory check of the accounts which Mr. Savins reluctantly provided, showed no discrepancy of funds from either of the two trust funds targeted for invasion. This led to the rather simple conclusion that pecuniary gain was not at the heart of the matter. When money is not the subject of crime, Watson, love, in its presence or its absence, usually is."

"But what of the ignominious death of the first clerk?"

"Camberley was apparently a fragile fellow with precious little to cling to," said Holmes. "Whether the secretary drove him to his death or not is a matter for the courts to decide. As for Fowler, I have sent him word by the evening post that the matter is has been resolved."

The Case of the Tainted Will

It has always seemed rather strange to me that of all the avocations available to a man of science and medicine, I should have become a scribbler. This is not said in derogation of the writing arts, but more in surprise that it should have taken hold of me. It is not an interest I would have thought to have pursued. I suppose that crime and its tangled mass of human suffering is not so far apace from the often-sanguine details of physical illness and disease. Perhaps it is after all the doctor in me that finds purpose in the observation and recording of human malefaction. My interest in such things was certainly increased by my erstwhile acquaintance with Mr. Sherlock Holmes, the noted London detective. What began for me as a simple arrangement for two Baker Street roommates, has become the nexus for several stories of greed, deceit, corruption, debauchery, and mayhem. I thank a good and benevolent God that my work as a physician is the counterbalance to the subversive burdens of criminal investigation to which I have been exposed.

One such investigation began in late spring of 18___. I had completed my rounds at St. Gregory's which took the better part of what was a chilly May morning. I returned to my office surgery to find a young street urchin sitting patiently in the very small parlor that served as anteroom for my modest practice. He was very poorly dressed, imperfectly washed, and offered by way of his personal space the unmistakable aroma of the river fisheries. Considering the pedestrian nature of my medical practice, it is undeniable that I had seen and treated many in his fraternity. He seemed troubled, but a sheepish smile offered an encouraging indication that he was a good lad. An early afternoon appointment having been cancelled, I ushered the young fellow into the surgery and began my conventional line of medical questioning, tempered accordingly by the patient's somewhat tender years.

I had only just begun to utter the first few inquiring formalities of the healer's monologue, when he interrupted me in a voice both imploring and sincere. I was far from 221B Baker Street and was not at the least prepared to hear matters of intrigue that were ordinary in those quarters and so extraordinary in these.

"You must save him, doctor," he blurted out with a sudden passion. "He's gone terrible ill, and bloody, and hardly has his breath about him, and when he does have it, he is moaning and gasping and....."

"Stop...stop!" I exclaimed with a commanding tone that only barely kept him from continuing. "Who must I save?" I asked, hoping to get some semblance of information from the young speaker who seemed now on the verge of hysteria.

"He is bleeding so, and burning with the fever, and his eyes all rolling about, and....."

His better sense had left him, and I grasped him by his shoulders and shook him gently to bring him round. Finally, the tempest of his narrative subsided, and he looked up at me with his eyes full of the innocent apology of a child.

"Now then," I continued with slow deliberation. "First off, tell me who it is that you speak of, and then explain what has happened and how you have come to know of it."

"He is a young gentleman. I've not but only seen him about. He's no account to me, but my lady is crying to bust apart over him. He's bleeding through his threads and she's crying and gasping awful, and I never have seen her acting such a way over nothing, and I'm worried she'll fall dead if I can't get no help for him, and that's just what she said she'll do if I can't bring him someone for doctoring. I sell my fishes hereabouts and I've seen folks come from your door with plasters on and bandages on and such, and so you must come for her sake...you must!"

"I want to believe your tale, my boy, but I need to be sure that you...." I stopped short in my plea for evidence when the youngster withdrew a fine linen handkerchief from his pocket stained with a considerable volume of blood that was barely congealed. The fine cloth was of a quality hardly common among fishing folk of the Thames. It was embroidered with the monogram "LHT."

"Your story rings true..., or true enough," I murmured almost to myself. A few moments later I was in a cab with the youth, rattling toward the riverside tenements that snaked themselves around the fetid shores of the Thames. The gentle descent to the river district belied another descent – one that marked a descent in wages, in lodgings, in furnishings, in food, and in favor. Here were the poor quarters of a rich city, where hard labor and hard lives mingled to nevertheless produce a hearty breed of Englishmen.

The cab rolled to the curb beside a long, unbroken line of shabby row houses. The boy bounded out, but I caught him up by the collar and had him lead me through an alley in the row, back finally to a low door in the face of a sodden wood frame dwelling house. In a side room that barely held a narrow table and a crooked cot, a smoking spirit lamp illuminated the figure of a young man in desperate straits. His injury was harsh, but not critical. I cleaned and dressed the wound and brought him to some comfort with a sleeping draught. My young office visitor went mum after a sharpened look from his young "lady," and the young woman herself refused to answer any of my questions. My threat to lodge a report with the local station did not seem to ruffle her determination. I learned nothing of the details surrounding the injury and was at a loss as to whether or how to proceed. I had no alternative but to leave bandages and medicines for the patient and return to my office.

Doctors are not officers of the law; their duty is a duty of care, not of consequence. My riverside patient was ill, and I performed the skills of my medical arts to set him right. The circumstances of a patient's life that do not impact their health, are not the business of the physician....and yet something of this incident rankled in me. It was not until the following morning that I decided to present the details of the troubling episode to Holmes and ask his opinion on the matter.

I cleared my day's calendar and traveled the well-known streets to my old lodgings at 221B. It was early and a moderate rain had begun to splatter the cab roof, so I stepped lively to the curb and plodded up the stairway to the door of the flat – a door at which I had never taken the trouble to knock despite my friend's rather Bohemian habits of dress and board. He was sitting at the small writing table with pen in hand poised above a small notepad.

"Good morning, Watson," he said turning briskly. "I was just this minute setting myself to send a note around to your office asking you to visit." He rose from the desk chair and surveyed me rather minutely. "But I see you have arrived *sine notitiam*. It also appears you have arrived as the result of some incident or other that has disturbed your characteristic settled presence of mind."

"Holmes," I said with an almost indignant warmth, "it is quite impossible for you to know anything about the matter I bring to you this morning. Why I just this moment entered the suite and have not uttered as much as a greeting."

"Forgive me my dear friend," he replied almost apologetically, "but I am an insufferable observer. I observe as unconsciously as others take breath. You must be aware after all the time we have known one another that for me observation is indomitable. For example, I observed a personal agitation in you the moment you crossed the doorsill. I know your domestic life is as steady as stone, so your upset is almost certainly some troubling circumstance of your medical practice." Holmes then strode across the room and stood almost uncomfortably close to me for a moment or two. "Also, I do not wish to give offence, Watson, but two particular studies of mine have been on the absorbent characteristics of Shetland wool, and the inherently porous quality of our English shoe leather. You see, both products effectively absorb the odors to which they are exposed. Leather heels and soles are veritable sponges for moisture, and the telltale aromas those moisture contain. Whatever we tread upon, leaves distinctive traces. And Shetland wool is a notorious retainer of odors. The interstices between the wool fibers are havens for odors, both pleasant and irksome. Notwithstanding your penchant for cleanliness, Watson, it is entirely safe to say that within the last 12 hours, your shoes and topcoat have come into contact with the moistures and odors of the riverside environs. Piscatory airs are particularly invasive, my friend. Finally, your personal visit to those unsavory sections of the city lead to the obvious conclusion that your visit there was on an emergency medical basis."

I did my best to conceal my reaction to Holmes's extraordinary skill at drawing precise and telling conclusions from commonplace observations, but even after years of exposure to his gifts, I stood there amazed. It was all I could do to look up from my shoes and my topcoat and say sheepishly, "You are quite correct...pray continue."

"The clues from your person end there, Watson, but the morning edition of *The Times* contains a lead story that completes the picture rather neatly."

I lifted the paper from the small table beside the divan and read the following under a sub-headline of the fourth column that ran, "Young MP Reported Missing: Foul Play Suspected"

Leonitus Theadore Haredon, recently elected member of the House of Lords, and son of Sir Andrew Haredon recently deceased, was reported missing Tuesday morning by his aunt, Lady Elizebeth Charist of Linnings Grove, Borwich. According to investigations by Scotland Yard, a gentleman matching Haredon's description was seen near the river front....

The paper slipped from my hand and fell to the floor. I turned guiltily to face Holmes, and the look of desperation written on my face must have been evident, for my friend read it in an instant.

"Do not trouble yourself, my good fellow," Holmes said reassuringly. "I am sure that you conducted yourself with the utmost propriety. But please, tell me precisely what transpired during your riverside housecall yesterday and be brief. In thirty minutes, Alexander Minier, an esteemed barrister from the offices of Stalworth and James, Esquires, should be arriving. He is the legal agent of the Haredon family, engaged specifically by Lady Charist, the aging aunt of your recent patient. From what I have heard of the man, he is both prompt and pompous."

I had made a mental record of my movements of the day earlier and left no point untold, howsoever trivial I might have thought it. My long experience with Holmes's methods had taught me no less. The detail of the monogrammed handkerchief convinced Holmes that my patient was in fact the young MP reported upon by the morning papers. When I concluded, the detective rejoined, "It is an interesting narrative, doctor, but a good deal more light needs to be shed upon the shadows in this matter."

Holmes had just finished urging Mrs. Hudson to hold the lunch board until after the expected guest had departed, when the bell on the street door was rung, and the barrister was ushered into the apartment. He was a man of fastidious dress and deportment. In short, his entire being proclaimed him a proud and esteemed member of London's legal tribe. He strode into the room with an imperious air and, seeing two men within, demanded which of us was Sherlock Holmes.

"I am Sherlock Holmes," my friend said coolly, "and this is my colleague and associ..." Holmes began to introduce me but was cut abruptly short by the stentorian voice of the barrister - a voice accustomed to being heard and regarded.

"My interest here does not extend to a 'colleague and associate,'" said Minier with an arrogant and condescending tone. He then looked at me intently and snarled, "Give us the room so that I may have a word with... 'the detective.'"

"Either Dr. Watson remains," Holmes said dispassionately, "or you can tell your client that 'the detective' has refused her case out of hand, a development that you – given your position of trust – may find difficult to explain. The choice is entirely yours." Holmes dropped into the armchair and reached for the morning pages of *The Times*. "And make up your mind presently; you have already interrupted my morning coffee."

Minier was no stranger to a harsh exchange. Years in the courtroom had hardened his character into an impenetrable shield; Holmes's response had no visible effect upon the man.

"My duty is to convey to you the details my client wishes you to be informed of," Minier snarled. "Before doing so, I will tell you frankly sir, that I believe her selection of you as an agent in this matter is utter foolishness. You are neither a member of the local police, nor of Scotland Yard, nor of any organized constabulary. You are, in essence, a meddler for hire. Your 'investigations' as the press is fond of referring to them, are mere sensational episodes of interference in legal matters that would have come to law and been resolved without your trifling. I have spoken at some length with an inspector at Scotland Yard, and while he persists in clinging somewhat to the reputation you have fabricated, I told him that professionally, you are little more than an amusing interlocutor."

I was aghast at this torrent of a diatribe, but if Holmes were affected in any way, he certainly did not show it. All the while he had been perusing the columns of *The Times*. When the barrister finally stopped speaking, my friend remained comfortably seated with an expression no less casual than if Mrs. Hudson had asked him to come to table for supper. He turned his head from the columns and looked at Minier with the slightest of a sardonic smile.

"My, but you are a troublesome fellow," Holmes remarked. "I suppose your exposure to the darkness of the legal world has left this bitter mark on you. Or perhaps you are simply a darkened creature by nature. In any event, will you kindly come to the business at hand? No doubt you are a busy man and wish to discharge yourself of your obligation here without further delay."

Minier was not prepared for this measured response. He was no doubt accustomed to addressing frightened souls standing in the dock, shivering in fear, or declaring legal technicalities to clients who hardly understood them. He stood stupidly silent for a moment, then collected himself stiffly, and turned to the matter of delivering to Holmes the information his client had instructed him to deliver.

"I represent the interests of Lady Elizebeth Charist," Minier began mechanically. "She is the widowed sister of Sir Andrew Haredon, recently deceased, and aunt to Leonitus

Theadore Haredon, currently a Member of Parliament. Sir Leo has been a missing person for the better part of three days, and his aunt wishes to engage your services to discover his whereabouts and return him to the embrace of his family."

? Are there no other family members," Holmes asked.

"Lady Charist is a widower and had no children. Her nephews are especially dear to her. Sir Leo has a younger brother, Peter, but aside from the boys' aunt, there are no other living relations. The boys' mother died soon after Peter's birth. Consequently, the Haredon line relies on the boys to continue the family lineage."

"Would you care to provide anything further?" Holmes inquired dispassionately.

"The two brothers have been effectively estranged for years," Minier continued. "They live under the same roof but have come to despise one another thoroughly, and their animosities have upon occasion risen to the level of personal injury. I am not in a position to pass judgment, but the younger Peter has made no secret of his hatred for *primogeniture*. He is a young man disposed to a wildness bordering on criminality, and his circle of acquaintances include several very unsavory characters. It would not be surprising to me to learn that Leo's disappearance is...." The barrister broke off suddenly, as though having come too close to revealing a thought not

43

appropriate to reveal. "That is the substance of my message to you from her Ladyship," the advocate said curtly, "and it concludes my business here." He turned to leave but was stopped by the commanding tone in Holmes's voice.

"You have just now described yourself as your Ladyship's messenger. That is ever so convenient. In that capacity," Holmes said with his characteristic charm and smile, "I wish you to deliver a message for me. Tell Her Ladyship I will need to speak with her on this matter at eight o'clock this evening at the family's town apartments... and one more thing," Holmes said, and paused before resuming, "Make certain she receives my message without delay."

This last instruction visibly rattled the advocate. His eyes bulged to round disks, and his face flushed a lovely shade of crimson. To his credit – if such men deserve any – he responded not at all and took his leave without retort.

The apartment door had barely closed upon our visitor, when Holmes assumed that smoldering concentration that belied his full engagement in a case. Mrs. Hudson was summoned and informed that Holmes and I would not be available for her excellent luncheon. It was a bit of news the faithful housekeeper was accustomed to hearing, but it invariably caused her to cast her usual sharp glance of irritation upon the two of us, and utter her customary reply, "As you wish, sir."

"Watson, you must revisit the wharves without delay and speak to young Leo, or at the very least, to the young woman who assisted him. You must not allow her to dismiss your inquiries. She will not speak to me, but she knows you are the doctor who saved him. Be persistent in this. If she will not relent, tell her that Sir Leo is in grave danger, and that only she can save him. His life may depend upon your success."

These instructions were delivered with the vigorous energy I had so often heard when the various moving parts of a case were set swirling in the detective's mind, challenging him to arrange them in a logical order. It was this reduction of chaos to order that was his animating spirit. I find it hard to admit, but at such times it was not uncommon for me to be quite uncertain regarding the exact details of the tasks that Holmes expected me to undertake.

"But what shall I ask? What do you need to know," I inquired.

"Certainly, the details of his injury are paramount," Holmes said. "And while you are about gathering that information, I will be doing some searching through the death records. In spite of his arrogance, what our recent visitor left unsaid, may have spoken more to the point than he knew. I think this matter may have connections that lie deeper than common assault and robbery. Let us return here no later than half past five to compare findings, shall we?"

"I made my way back to the wood-framed house in the twisted maze of dwellings at the river's edge. Leo Haredon had left only minutes before my arrival. Grace was the name of the young woman of the house who had assisted me with the patient. Surprisingly, she showered me with thanks, offered a cup of tea, and seemed genuinely anxious to share her story and that of the Young Haredon. As it happens, she was the daughter of a prominent London merchant whose business collapsed under her father's misdeeds, leaving her family little more than early death or utter ruin. Her life was now relegated to servile work in a riverside pub, and her reputation for kindness drew occasional homeless lads to her door. She knew Leo Haredon in her earlier life, and they formed a friendship that neither poverty nor tragic changes of fortune could ever break. He helped her as much as her pride would allow, but the disgrace of her father's crimes often kept the two of them apart in a culture that does not understand misfortune and does not forgive it. She related the details of the incident with clarity colored by an evident personal concern for her friend.

It seems that on the evening of a recent visit to Grace, Haredon had been attacked in one of the dark alleys. The attacker was a short, stocky tough, apparently one of the many river rats that crawled about the wharves to take whatever could be taken with a voice of sneering demand and the flash of a knife blade.

"Grace, my dear girl," I urged, "... tell me as many of the details as you can. This incident with Sir Leo may have repercussions that we least expect. Please, be precise!"

"There is little I can add to what Leo told me directly, doctor. The man approached him with knife drawn, raised his hand, and proceeded to.... Oh, it is a horror to me still. I can hardly speak the words to describe it."

"You say the man moved immediately to the attack? Didn't he first demand money or wallet or watch? Weren't any of Sir Leo's valuables taken from him? Was he even robbed, then?"

"Leo remarked that very same thing, Doctor. Why would a criminal approach a well-dressed gentleman, take the risk of being charged with assault... or worse, and yet leave the injured victim with all his possessions untouched?"

"Did Sir Leo defend himself, or was he taken unawares," I asked.

"Oh yes, Doctor, Leo fought back quite bravely. He said he was almost able to disarm the man, and had he not fought so, the injury to his lower shoulder would have been more grave. He claims the fellow would almost certainly have... it would have been the end of him. Thank God he was able to stumble to my door, and I cared for him as best I could through the night, though I was in a bad way with worrying over him. In the morning, Leo was lying quietly, but the stillness frightened me. I must have been close to hysterical when I sent Tim to summon a doctor, and thankfully you arrived, and all was made well. When Leo left this morning, he was weakened, but able and alert. He asked me to keep the incident to myself, but you were his very good saving angel, Doctor, and I trust that you will not use my relation of the incident to do him any harm."

The young woman spoke with a sincerity I could not question. For Holmes's sake, I did my best to keep the telling details of her narrative uppermost in my memory.

I returned to Baker Street at the appointed time, and Holmes joined me there not five minutes after I arrived. I shared with him all the particulars of my encounter with Grace, and was sure to delineate the facts with precision, knowing all too well his penchant for details and specification. He seemed remarkably satisfied with my account, especially regarding the matter of the attack itself, and the unusual circumstance of the perpetrator having left the scene without any of the spoils of his criminal undertaking. When I asked Holmes why it was that he appeared most curious about that specific feature of the attack, he appeared thoughtful for a moment, then explained,

"It is curious, indeed. There are a goodly number of possibilities that present themselves in light of that singular fact, Watson, but we should not run towards conclusions until there is a sufficiency of evidence to give them secure foundation. In any event, unless my notions of this business are very far afield, I believe we are approaching that sufficiency."

"And has your research with the death records yielded any fruit?" I inquired.

"Unfortunately, that was not time well spent, Watson. I was interested in reading the last will and testament of Sir Leo's father, the late Sir Andrew Haredon. As you may be aware, the Court of Probate maintains scrupulous files of all wills and testaments that have been carried through the British probate process. It is a streak of bad luck for us that Sir Andrew's will has not yet been submitted for proving, so the document is not on file with the court," Holmes said musingly. "However, that fact is strange in itself, considering that Sir Andrew's passing occurred more than a year ago," he said in a voice that trailed off toward some thought that appeared to trouble him.

"Is the hiatus in submitting the will for review a relevant fact," I asked.

"I cannot yet be sure that that is of specific importance, but it certainly may have weight here – weight that may inform us further regarding the unfortunate matter of our young Leo's attack.

"But then, where are we left, and what is to be done? The young lord's safety may be hanging by a thread," I said worriedly.

"I do not believe he is in any immediate danger. The attack on the wharves might have been a mere chance encounter with a desperate vagabond, or it may have been a surreptitious incident, filled with the animus of an unknown and villainous enemy. If it is the latter, I doubt that another attempt so close upon the first will be undertaken. Sir Leo is safe for now, but I fear there is a malefactor afoot."

"But Holmes, what do you think of this Peter Haredon, younger brother of Sir Leo?" I continued. "Minier spoke very strongly against him, and I must admit, if memory serves, his name has been no stranger to the papers in the past few years. The columns make him out to be a fellow who has driven close to the criminal edge on more than one occasion. Certainly, he is no paragon, Holmes. To hear Minier speak of him, you would think the fellow has barely escaped hanging."

"Minier certainly has experience with the stock of English criminals," Holmes ruminated with a slow consideration. "...and the picture he painted of the younger Haredon, combined with your unflattering memories from the newsprint, are clearly unsettling. And yet, when I consider the entire accounting as it now stands, there are numbers here, my dear Watson, that do not reconcile to my satisfaction. Something is amiss. Perhaps the encounter this evening with Lady Charist will enlighten us. Until then, our luncheon, having been most regrettably neglected, I suggest we partake of some cold roast from the sideboard with a short glass of port, and refresh our appetites. I haven't the courage to try the patience of Mrs. Hudson with requesting the preparation of yet another unscheduled supper."

*　　*　　*

When we had completed our rather inadequate evening meal, Holmes withdrew a ponderous volume from his bookshelves titled, *Charland's Hornbook of British Probate Law,* and he proceeded to immerse himself in the index and among its thousand pages of regulations. At half seven, we gathered ourselves and departed for the luxurious in-town lodgings of the Haredon family.

A formal butler, admittedly a striking contrast to our Baker Street boy in buttons, opened the door and led us into a parlor whose furnishings and decor bespoke the wealth of a very old English family of position. In a few moments, Lady Charist entered, bid us be seated, and after exchanging brief introductions and greetings, moved with unexpected informality, to the matter at hand.

"Thank you for accepting the engagement in this matter, Mr. Holmes," she said mildly. "I fear I may have to apologize for the rash behaviors of my advocate, Mr. Minier. I know that he often has difficulty surrendering the aggressions of the courtroom when he is among us laymen and women."

"The man's behavior was a mere trifle. Pray continue," Holmes rejoined politely.

"As to the matter of your services, please calculate your fees and disbursements and I will arrange for payment without delay. I am so happy to relate that Leo has returned home within the hour and he is resting comfortably in his room upstairs. I would have sent word to you and saved you the trouble of the travel across town, but he is only just recently returned, and a note could not have been delivered to you in time. Be sure to add travel time to your bill of fees and know that full endorsement will be promptly accomplished. I thank you again for your engagement."

"May I presume you are aware that Sir Leo was injured rather grievously," Holmes asked.

"Oh yes, Mr. Holmes. It was a terribly nasty business. I was utterly beside myself until he assured me that he had been thoroughly examined and treated by a medical professional. Traveling to certain quarters of the city is a foolish and presumptuous risk. Leo insists on visiting a friend who has fallen on hard times. The boy has such endearing sensibilities, and I admire him his tender feelings, but he needs to be more discreet. I only thank God he is restored to health. And so, I hope that is an end to the matter... unless you have anything further?"

"Lady Charist," Holmes said with notable concern, "I have reason to believe that Sir Leo's injury may have been part of an intrigue with implications beyond a mere street crime. Do you know of anyone who might wish him ill? I realize his position as MP invariably attracts political enemies, but is there anyone who might bear some personal animosity?

The question struck her like an arrow. Surely the hatred between the brothers came immediately to her mind and displayed itself in her troubled features and her suddenly nervous carriage. Holmes and I exchanged a knowing glance. It was several moments before she could compose herself to reply.

"I can think of no one who bears him any serious degree of malice, Mr. Holmes. You must excuse me, but I am not quite myself since this disturbing business began. I thank you again for your pains on behalf of my family," and she rose and moved graciously out of the room. The butler must have been otherwise engaged, and Holmes and I stepped out of the parlor and into the large foyer where a sweeping staircase curled down from the upper floor and led toward the entrance doors to the street. As we gained the doors, a man's voice, weak but imperative, summoned us from the staircase. It was Sir Leo in a dressing gown and slippers.

"Gentlemen," he said cordially, glancing left and right to be sure no one was about, "a word...in the library, if you please," and he pointed with the finger of his left arm to the double doors directly opposite the parlor. His right arm was set in a linen sling to relieve the weight of the limb from the recovering shoulder wound.

The three of us moved into the spacious room where three walls were covered entirely with floor to ceiling bookshelves. I could see Holmes eyes devouring the stacks of volumes hungrily. Haredon stopped just inside the closed doors, looked closely at me, and gave a start.

"You...you were there," he stammered. "You were with Grace at the river. I don't understand...how is this possible," and his voice trailed off in a mumble of half-formed words.

"Lord Haredon," I quickly replied. "You are quite correct. I was with Grace. My name is Dr. John Watson. I dressed your wounds and gave you a sleeping draught to calm you. I hope you are feeling better. Grace's young lad Tim fetched me quite by luck and I followed him to the wharves to look in on you." I could see he was puzzled by it all, so I was very much relieved when Holmes came forward and explained the strange coincidence that had brought his aunt's detective and his bedside physician together at his home. After but a few moments of my friend's clear and frank discourse, the unexpected string of events were sorted out and put right.

"Mr. Holmes," he said finally, "I am anxious to speak with you regarding a particular aspect of my recent injury. That evening, I was attacked suddenly and without provocation. It has troubled me that robbery was not the primary motive. The few valuables I had on my person I would have gladly surrendered to the thief, but they were neither demanded nor taken from me after I was wounded. Apparently, the blackguard sought only to take my life. I realize I am an official of Her Majesty's government, but at this early stage of my career, my political positions are hardly radical, so a political enemy bent upon my death is unthinkable. I wonder if you have any insight into why my life would be worth taking for its own sake?

"The question you raise is the very same one I have asked myself," replied Holmes. "I have two theories; I will share one with you at this time, and, begging your pardon, I shall keep the other to myself until I have secured further facts." Holmes voice lowered and his tone became thoughtful and confidential. "May I be frank, Sir Leo... even if that frankness might implicate someone dear to you?"

"If being frank will help clear this business, then all else be damned. Yes, Mr. Holmes, by all means, be frank."

"Very well," Holmes rejoined. "It is common knowledge that your brother, Peter, is openly resentful of your ranking as the eldest son and first in line for the Haredon inheritance. It is similarly well known that he is a man given to antagonistic and reckless behaviors, some of which have resulted in criminal entanglements. Forgive me for being presumptuous in this regard, but do you believe your brother could be involved in some way with your injury by the riverfront?"

"I am very sorry to say that you have good reason to ask the question, Mr. Holmes, but my answer is no. It is quite true that Peter is very resentful about my being the eldest son and entitled to the lion's share of the family wealth. Yes, he has had criminal episodes and scrapes with the law for years and is of a hot and combative disposition. I hate how my brother lives, Mr. Holmes, and I hate how he treats others. I hate that he hates my ascendancy over him, and yet... he is my brother, and I love him, and I know in my heart and soul he would never harm me in any way."

"If what you say is true, Sir Leo, then I am left with but one explanation, and as I have often remarked to Dr. Watson, when all other theories of a case have been eliminated, the one remaining, howsoever improbable, is the solution." Holmes buttoned the front of his Mackinaw and appeared ready to make an exit, when he turned to Lord Haredon and asked casually, "Would you happen to have a duplicate copy of your father's last will and testament? It need not be a conformed copy. A simple duplicate will serve."

Sir Leo produced the document, and after Holmes gave assurance it would be speedily returned and treated with all possible discretion, we took our leave. I knew from long experience, that when my friend was ruminating on some theory of the case, it was best to leave him with his thoughts, and so the drive to Baker Street was completed without the distractions of conversation.

The following day was bright and clear, a genuine treasure for late spring in England's capital city. I had spent the morning and the larger part of the afternoon attending to the medical duties imposed upon me by my professional life. When the surgery finally cleared, a message arrived from Holmes asking if I might join him and Inspector Lestrade at Baker Street at eight o'clock. Anxious to learn of any developments in Sir Leo's case, I accepted, and when the three of us were assembled at 221b, Holmes made what I considered to be a rather singular request.

"I am expecting a visitor," he said with his characteristic dispassion, "and I wish the two of you to act as witnesses *invisibilis*. It is only necessary that you hear what my visitor has to say, and that you can attest to what you have heard. If my impressions of him are correct, he will divulge matters of high importance. His identity will be made perfectly clear to you, and you may present yourselves, confront him, and speak with him freely after you hear me utter the phrase, 'Pride goeth before the fall.' Do either of you have any questions?" he finally asked and looked at us as a teacher might when looking at students who may have missed some important point in lecture.

Lestrade and I stared at each other, then stared at Holmes, but the inspector and I had both been long subjected to the unorthodox methods of the man, so we agreed by silent acquiescence and awaited further instruction.

"If you both will be so kind as to step into the lavatory," he explained, "and keep the door sufficiently ajar to hear and perhaps see the goings on with our guest, you will be able to discharge yourselves of your obligation."

Close upon the appointed time of the visitor's arrival, Lestrade and I installed ourselves accordingly and waited upon the implementation of our secret service. Holmes was lounging comfortably in the hearth-side armchair, as Mrs. Hudson was laying tea service for two on the sideboard along with a small tray of almond biscuits. "Thank you, Mrs. Hudson," Holmes said patiently, "I am sorry to trouble you this late after the supper hour, but I am expecting a visitor, and I must keep up at least the appearances of cordiality."

"It is no trouble, Mr. Holmes," she replied with a slight shortness in her voice, "but a bit more advance notice of your needs would be appreciated, sir," and as she opened the door to retreat, the bell was heard at the entrance door. A moment later, a very well-dressed gentleman appeared in the open doorway of the flat.

"Barrister," Holmes said in a loud and cheerful voice, "do come in and make yourself comfortable. I have taken the liberty of putting out some tea and biscuits, so please do partake."

As Lestrade and I stood quietly in the darkened lavatory, I could see and hear the advocate clearly. Albert Minier did not smile at his host, offer his hand, or remove his hat. "I am not interested in socializing," Minier said with a snarl. "I am here because my client has asked me to speak with you on a matter touching upon the injury to her nephew. I wish to do so and exit immediately thereafter. I have no interest in spending any more time than is necessary with a 'detective.'"

"Very well then," Holmes said slowly, "certainly let us get on to the matter at hand so that you are not unnecessarily detained. You may be interested to know that I have visited and spoken at length to Sir Leo Haredon. You should also know that I procured a duplicate copy of Sir Albert Haredon's last will and testament – the very document that you prepared as his barrister. As you know, the 14th provision of that will provides language that creates the 'Haredon Foundation.' The structure of the Foundation is left rather clouded, but a careful reading reveals that the powers reserved to the Foundation's president are sweeping, to say the least. In fact, as the language is written, the president has unrestricted fiscal powers over all expenditures, and none of the president's actions are subject to the review of any board or any court. Legal documents can often be opaque, and Andrew Haredon's will is no exception. However, a scrupulous review usually yields clarity. Provision 14 grants unfettered authorities to the named president of the Foundation.... and the named president is you, sir."

At this point, Holmes was almost surprised to see that the words he had spoken thus far were not disturbing the barrister's presence of mind in the least. Minier seemed almost amused.

"The will goes on to explain," Holmes continued, "that Provision 14 will take effect only upon the death of the primary beneficiary, Sir Leo Haredon. Restated in the simplest of layman's terms," Holmes said casually, "if Sir Leo were to die young...... you would become a very wealthy man."

Minier stood by stoically and searched Holmes's face with a lawyer's eyes, looking for a weakness, or a bluff, or a lingering hint of uncertainty. He saw none.

Holmes did not relent. "Using your extensive knowledge of London's criminal underworld, you arranged for what would have appeared to be the chance murder of a gentleman who was known by many to be a frequent visitor to the wharves. You knew the public was aware of the criminal inclinations of Peter Haredon, and his anger against the eldest son's privilege under British law. Having Peter arrested, and prosecuting him as conspiring to kill his brother, would have been a relatively simple matter for a man in your position. With one brother dead, the other in prison, and an aging aunt, the will that you had authored to your own benefit would effectively deliver to you the entire family fortune. As things stand presently," Holmes opined and carelessly reached for his pipe and pouch, "you will be disbarred, charged with conspiracy to commit murder, and summarily imprisoned.

"Minier removed his hat, slid into the comfort of the divan, and smiled broadly. "You are not an intelligent man, Holmes, but you are clever," he said almost good-naturedly. "Clever does not win the day my friend, intelligence does. I will never be saddled with this crime you speak of. The labyrinth of details I arranged in furtherance of Leo's murder could never be untangled and never be brought back to me. You are a local drudge and cannot command the resources needed to connect a man of my standing to this crime. It would take you a lifetime, and even then, you would fail. I will admit that your assessment of the matter is surprisingly accurate. Bravo, monsieur detective. Unfortunately, there is nothing at all you can do to prove my involvement."

"What would you say," Holmes replied, "if I were to reveal to Lady Charist the open and frank admissions of guilt that you have just made to me here this evening?"

"My poor fellow," Minier answered almost laughing, "I would simply explain to Her Ladyship that you failed to solve the case, and in a desperate attempt to restore your undeserved reputation for solving crime, you have concocted this elaborate and absurd narrative against a man who ruffled your professional feathers. I must say, I am pleasantly surprised," Minier added, rising from the divan and lifting his hat to his head. "I had not expected to be so interestingly entertained this evening. I bid you good night."

"I do not know if you are a religious man," Holmes said as Minier was moving towards the door, "but are your familiar with Proverbs, chapter 16, verse 18?"

"I most assuredly am not," Minier said distractedly, "but I suspect you will enlighten me."

"Yes, I will," Holmes returned with some little irony in his voice. "Pride goeth before the fall."

Those words were our cue, and Inspector Lestrade and I stepped through the lavatory door and into the room where Holmes remained seated, lighting his clay pipe with a flaming wooden match. Minier, simply startled at first, finally stared at us as though we were ghosts.

Inspector Lestrade was the first to speak.

"It may be I agreed with a few of the cruel things you said to me about Mr. Holmes here, but Mr. Holmes is a sight more clever than you give him credit for. I heard enough from you tonight, Barrister Minier, to swear out a complaint against you, sir. And as for untangling your 'labyrinth of details," well Mr. Holmes here may not have the time for such things, but Scotland Yard does, and it would be our pleasure to untangle them against you, sir."

In short order, the barrister was manacled and led out of the room by the stalwart Lestrade. Holmes carried the cumbersome tome of *Charland's Hornbook of British Probate Law* from the writing table to the shelves alongside the window box, and with pipe clenched securely in his teeth, he carefully nestled the volume into the open slot among its fellows.

The Case of the Treasured Book

The Wednesday morning hours in my surgery, ordinarily dedicated to the relatively modest number of patients seeking my attention, were unexpectedly silent. A late-night storm had moved across the city and deposited a thick coating of ice on cobblestones, flagstones, alleys, and stairs. For a workday morning in London, the street outside my small office was eerily quiet. I was taking the opportunity of the respite to complete some neglected paperwork, when I heard the footfalls of a team of dray horses pulling what must have been a very heavy carriage. A quick glance through my streetside office window confirmed my speculation, as a large police wagon was drawn to the curb and an officer, fending off the chill temperatures under a heavy police cloak with a high collar, came carefully up the ice-encrusted stairs and rang the office bell.

Once the imposing figure was sufficiently unwrapped and the winter garb hung upon the rack, I was able to identify the visitor as Inspector Lestrade of Scotland Yard. It was no small surprise to see Lestrade standing in the foyer of my surgery. His presence there was certainly incongruous. It is true I occasionally assisted the noted London detective, Mr. Sherlock Holmes, with his criminal investigations, and I was well acquainted with Lestrade in that capacity, but he had never before appeared at my office, and I looked at him rather dumbstruck. Finally, I greeted and welcomed him politely and did my best to overcome what must have been my evident surprise at his presence in my medical workspace. I stepped into my office reception area and asked him to come through.

"May I offer you a very hot cup of tea on this cold morning?" I asked genially. "This storm has left the streets in a glaze of ice."

"With all of them slips and falls about it, Doctor, I should think it will be a boon for your doctoring skills," he said good-naturedly, but when he saw that I was not at all amused by the remark, his smile faded quickly and was replaced by the ageless and doleful expression of the policeman at work. With business-like courtesy and a stiffened formality, he declined my offer of tea.

"It is best I come to the point, doctor," he said. "We are holding a prisoner at the Yard, and he is feeling ill to be sure, and if you would be so kind as to step over to see him, Doctor, the Yard would be very appreciating, sir."

"And what of the Yard's regular surgeon on premises," I asked. "I believe his name is Ackles...Dr. William Ackles. Has he been pensioned... is he unavailable?"

"Dr. Ackles has not taken his retirement leave, sir, and he remains 'with the Yard,' but he is not the man for this bit of work, Doctor," the inspector said with that hesitant modulation of voice heard when a speaker prefers to keep some things unspoken.

"I do not understand, inspector. Dr. Ackles is a very competent physician. Whatever do you mean by saying he is 'not the man for this bit of work?' What kind of work are you referring to, Lestrade?"

The inspector cleared his throat, and with that same hesitation in his voice, he stammered, "Well..., you may as well know going in... the prisoner has asked for you directly... by name, sir"

I was certainly not prepared for this disarming revelation. With the rare exception of my work with Holmes, I was not in the habit of mingling with common criminals, and even my many connections with Holmes's cases seldom brought my identity into focus for the official record.

"Who is this prisoner," I demanded of Lestrade.

"At the present time he is only a suspect, Doctor Watson, and so his name is not for the information of the public at large, sir."

"Without his name and some particulars of the man, I will not accompany you, Inspector," I said sternly, "and I am hardly a member of 'the public at large' when you come to my place of business and ask me to become entangled in a Scotland Yard investigation."

Lestrade looked sheepishly about before responding. "His name is Michaels....Geoffrey Michaels. He's near your age, Doctor, of a medium build with a short flat nose and a head full of silvery white hair. More than that, doctor, I am not at 'liberties' to share. Do you know him then?" Lestrade asked hopefully.

The name and description immediately connected to an old memory. Michaels was a medical student with me at university. He was an ever-smiling, rambunctious and spirited fellow, laughing and joking his way through his studies while the rest of us were morose and worried in every term. He regularly posted the highest grades and was accounted one of the brightest lights of the class, destined for preferred practice or a serious research berth. Even as a young man, his hair was as silver white as snow. We were friends, though not quite friendly enough to have kept up the acquaintance after our studies came to an end. Nonetheless, the very thought that he was sitting in a subterranean prison cell at Scotland Yard was intolerable. I knew my morning patients would never brave the frozen streets to keep appointments they would happily have cancelled upon the slightest excuse, so I ushered Lestrade hurriedly out of the surgery, clambered into the police wagon with him, and suffered the hard ride on the icy streets to the Yard.

The mid-morning sun was slowly warming the ice slick into a muddy slush as we approached the dark structure of the Scotland Yard station. After the perfunctory clearances had been accomplished, I was taken into the building's depths and found myself in a small damp cell standing before a very older version of a lad I once knew. He was seated on a narrow wall-mounted shelf that served as a bed, and his sluggish posture was the first signal that he was a broken version of the man I had cavorted with at university. I was loath to admit it to myself, but my professional eye glimpsed the telltale signs of a man who was accustomed to either the relentless ingestion of alcohol, or to the debilitating influences of long-term narcotics use.

"Dr. John Watson, if I am correct," he said in a dreamy, listless voice. "You are certainly older, but your mien and carriage remain unmistakable. I knew that you were still alive, but I calculated the chances that you would actually come to see me at something substantially less than 50 percent."

As he muttered these words, he neither lifted a hand in greeting, nor rose to address me firsthand. The vivacity and charm of his former self had disappeared entirely. No doubt he had traveled some difficult roads in the years since our studies, and they had taken his pleasant manner and genial disposition and hardened them beyond recognition. He looked up at me and his lips tightened into a wry smile, and when he finally spoke, his voice was bitter and cynical. "It looks as though you have done rather well for yourself," he said sarcastically. "Oh now, don't look all put upon," he said as I felt myself flush a bit. "Your success is actually a comfort to me," and he pulled himself up to a sitting position on the cot, although he still slouched lazily against the wall. "I am sure that by this time you are wondering to yourself, 'What in blazes could this ruined pathetic fellow want with the likes of me?'"

"I am 'wondering' no such thing," I admonished him, and yet I could not help but admit that he was in large part correct. I had come to offer solace to an old medical comrade and found myself instead on the receiving end of discourtesy and provocation. My patience was waning, and Michaels –

still well in possession of a uniquely insightful mind – sensed my discomfort.

"For the sake of our old acquaintance and for your kindness in responding to my unexpected summons, I will come to the point summarily," he muttered in a tired monotone. "Within 48 hours I will be released from custody as a result of the efforts of some of London's finest legal talent. It is an unremarkable certainty that within one week of my release, I shall be found dead. The people with whom I have done business these 20 years past do not leave potentially troublesome matters unresolved. My possessions are few, and of those, books are my only treasures. They are what good is left of an ill-spent life," he said coldly. He turned about and faced me for the first time, and said with decision, "John, you must take my copy of Henry Gray's *Anatomy of the Human Body*. Tell me – please tell me now – that you will take my copy of Gray."

"I do not understand any of this, Michaels," I exclaimed excitedly. "You are speaking nonsense! Your release – your death – your old textbook – these are the ramblings of a mind overborne, old chap. Come now...take hold of yourself," and I sat down beside him and placed my hand firmly on his shoulder. His frame shuddered slightly but to his credit, he did not succumb to his emotion.

"You must take it," he repeated desperately in a raised voice. "Tell me you will... for the love of God, man, tell me you will do this one thing for me." The heated animation that had come into him upon the subject of the book left me no choice but to calm him with my assurance that I would do as he wished.

In a few moments he had relapsed into his previous lethargy. We exchanged the formalities of departure appropriate to the unusual circumstances, and I quit Michaels's cell. The subterranean levels of the Scotland Yard station are unwholesome places. The air is heavy with a dampness almost viscous, and if odors told tales, many chapters of evil-doing and hopelessness were there for the telling. As I threw sidelong glances into the long row of cell doors adjoining Michaels's, I could see shadows of men huddled on the same low shelves upon which I had just been reclined. In the cell adjacent to Michaels's, two ragged, bearded, hunched up ruins of men stood leaning heavily against the bars looking out at me as I passed along in my fine wool topcoat, pressed trousers, and brushed hat. One of them spat at my feet and cursed me with a blasphemous remark so foul I dare not repeat it on these pages. I moved to the corridor's end with my uniformed escort and was accompanied to Lestrade's office, where I recounted to him the details of my conversation with the prisoner. The inspector seemed disappointed by my account. I am sure he had hopes of Michaels confiding in me and sharing some dark secrets of crimes that the Crown could take to law. In spite of my not accomplishing the anticipated task, Lestrade grudgingly agreed to accompany me to the prisoner's lodgings so I could legally take possession of the anatomy text that Michaels had so vigorously demanded of me.

We traveled across the muddied streets to a section of the city that could only be described as unsavory. Michaels's apartment was a rather shabby set of small, connected rooms commonly referred to as a "railroad flat." They seemed hardly a proper lodging for a man of Michaels's considerable intellect. The book was sitting on a low shelf alongside several other medical tomes. I had forgotten the unwieldy size and ponderous weight of the volume that I had carried with me so lightly through my years of medical study. It occurred to me how youth so carelessly lift and carries the heavy burdens of lifts, while age complains of them at every possible turn.

Lestrade insisted on looking through the book for letters, or notes that might be applied as evidence in the case. He took the volume, leafed through its pages with his thumb, then grasping it by the binding, gave it a hearty shaking, for the purpose no doubt, of dislodging any incriminating papers. He looked over at me finally and declared, "There are notes in handwriting along all the edges of the pages, doctor. What do you make of that?"

"It is a medical school textbook, Lestrade," I explained with an exaggerated simplicity. "Such marginal notes cover the pages of almost every medical text, every law text, and every engineering text I have ever seen. Michaels was a student once, and handwritten side-notes are what students write in their textbooks."

Lestrade uttered an inconsequential grunt *soto voce,* and when he was satisfied that no telltale memos were stuck between the pages, he permitted me to resume physical possession of the book. I carried it back to my office and gratefully deposited its bulk on the small table inside the entrance door.

The episode at the Yard with Michaels had troubled me. I am no stranger to the outbursts, whimsies, and delusions of my fellowmen. My years as a soldier and physician exposed me to every possible scene in the sad drama of the human situation. And yet, all those experiences did not contain an episode as disturbing as this. Here was a man, once young and hale, endowed with immeasurable natural gifts and a personality brimming with friendship and good will, now reduced to anger, bitterness, and cynicism. What kind of turn must such a fellow have made? These thoughts moved quickly and uneasily through my mind. And yet, in a moment or two, they were replaced seamlessly by the more immediate demands of my unfinished paperwork, unseen patients, and my luncheon, which, as a result of Lestrade's interruption, had been neglected one hour past its appointed time. For this reason, it was more than mere casual irritation when the office bell rang and promised to delay my midday meal even longer.

As was customary for patients, the visitor had rung and moved directly into the foyer that served as the practice intake station. The reception nurse, familiar with the visitor from many previous encounters, instructed him to go through, and I was pleasantly surprised to see Sherlock Holmes standing before me, somewhat muddied by the conditions of the street, but otherwise his thoroughly composed and confidently austere self.

"Good afternoon, Watson," he said cordially. "This weather is a dastardly mess. The city is awash in mud and slush. I fear I have soiled your carpeting beyond any reasonable degree of sanitation."

It is only dirt, Holmes," I remarked, "and dirt can always be swept and brushed and washed away and all made clean again."

"Would that it were so in all things, my friend," he said. "But let me come to the purpose of my visit. I was hoping I could impose to borrow of one of your books. It always seems the one book I most desperately need is the very one my library is without. Why do you suppose we never seem to have the one thing we need when we need it most, Watson?" he asked musing. "Surely this is a great mystery – one of those little life ironies, the true meanings of which are not meant to be revealed to us until the life hereafter."

"I was unaware that you were a believer in the 'hereafter,' Holmes," I said casually.

"We are imposed upon by the exigencies of the unknown to believe what seems comforting to us, are we not, my friend? I cannot claim to be one who harbors a 'faith,' or a 'belief' *per se*, but there is in us all a lingering, almost worrisome, 'hope,' is there not, Watson? The bard instructs us well, I think, when he states that "... conscience does make cowards of us all.""

It was not uncommon for Holmes to wax philosophic upon the slightest provocation, so I was not in the least surprised by his lofty remarks on the idea of life after death and what it might offer us mortals by way of enlightenment.

"Well, I am honored by your request to borrow one of my books, although I cannot think any of my titles would interest you. I have little more than shelves full of stuffy medical offerings. What would you have?" I asked, always anxious to be of service to him.

"I wonder," he rejoined with perfect equanimity, "if you might have a spare copy of Henry Gray's *Anatomy of the Human Body?*"

I was thoroughly startled. How could this be? How could Holmes possibly know of my very recent connection to the book? Could it be mere coincidence? Could Holmes actually need a copy of the very same book that was at the epicenter of my morning encounter at Scotland Yard? The obvious answer was, no! My long acquaintance with Holmes, and my exposure to his skillful, almost flawless intuition, made the very idea of coincidence the most remote of possibilities. Somehow, he knew the significance of the volume, and yet, I was resolved – I was determined – not to appear amazed or even affected by his petition. I assumed a look of sheer indifference and did my best to conceal all indications of surprise. I turned toward him in the most casual way and asked in a voice I thought was convincingly nonchalant, why he had interest in that particular text.

Holmes hesitated a long moment, then looked at me with a broadening and what seemed to be a pitying smile. "It was a great day for the English theater when you decided to become a doctor rather than pursue the Thespian arts, dear Watson. Had you not done so, you and your lovely bride would surely have lived a life of destitution. Your attempt just now to feign ignorance of the book's significance runs decidedly counter to the integrity and natural honesty in your nature, my friend. As an actor, you are an unmitigated failure."

"Holmes," I sputtered almost angrily, "You must have spoken to Lestrade then, and he has told you about the book. Or..., or perhaps you have been following my movements and were able to detect the title of the volume with your ship's glass. In any event," I said with some desperation, "you must be involved in some way with the case of Geoffrey Michaels's imprisonment."

"I have neither seen nor spoken with the inspector at any time in the last three days," he replied blandly, "nor have I been following your movements about town. Also, you should know that I was familiar with the significance of the book even before I saw it lying conspicuously on your foyer table a moment ago. As for my involvement in a case, you may be interested to know that I have been engaged by Sir Richard Norton, High Commissioner of the London Custom

House, on a matter that has been consuming all of my energies. It is a very tangled affair."

"Holmes, you are inexplicably inscrutable," I exclaimed. "If a new case is consuming all your energies, how the deuce have you divined the title of a book of which you cannot possibly know the significance?"

"Gracious me," Holmes exclaimed in a tone pretending to have taken great offence. "I am not accustomed to hearing you swear an oath, my friend. For you to have uttered the expression, 'how the deuce,' you must have been in a state of high agitation. You are not a man easily given to strong language," he continued with a sly smile. I fear that, gone unchecked, you might eventually be inclined to utter still stronger language, perhaps something as atrocious as _____, _____, _____."

I heard Holmes's words, and they were shockingly profane, but even more strange was their being the very same words and spoken in the very same accent and cadence as the hunched, unwashed criminal that spat at my feet from the cell adjacent to Geoffrey Michael's. In hardly the time it took me to hear and process the profanities, I realized that Holmes, in one of his many convincing disguises, was the vagabond who had accosted me from his cell, and hurled those detestable words as I passed down the corridor in the Scotland Yard cell-block. What purpose he had for playing such a role in that gruesome environment at the very same moment of my presence there, was beyond my understanding. I looked up at him from my seat and saw what I thought was a glimmer of apology around the edges of his sly smile.

"I can see from your expression, dear Doctor, that my little ruse has been brought to light by your keen eye and sagacious ear. No doubt you are wondering 'how the deuce' I was installed in a prison cell alongside your old school chum, Geoffrey Michaels. The circumstances of my presence there are parts of a dangerous story that I wish to share with you, Watson..., if you have the time to hear them..., and if the unkind words I hurled at you from my jail cell have not damaged our friendship or association." Holmes now reclined into the office chair adjoining mine and waited patiently upon my reply.

"You are a man of many talents, Holmes" I began slowly, "and I know from experience that you put them all to very good purpose. Occasionally, those purposes remain a mystery to the very practical sensibilities of an old sawbones such as myself. But that mystery is of no consequence. I am yours in friendship and association for as long as you have need of me. This morning's stormy weather has left my practice in pause. Pray, relate your 'dangerous story' and assure yourself of my assistance in it."

Holmes appeared genuinely relived by my assertions, and after joining me in a spare luncheon meal, he rose from his chair, and striding casually about the surgery, related a general outline of the "dangerous story" to which he had referred.

It seems that Geoffrey Michaels, the smiling, bright-light student of my university days, had fallen early into a life of easy criminal earnings and chemical dependency. Opium-laced cigarettes has started his decline. He had succumbed to the seductive fantasies of the drug and followed it still further into its stronger derivative compounds until he was hopelessly addicted. Sadly, his criminal life followed close upon his dependency. As a man with intimate knowledge of science and laboratory procedures, Michaels represented enormous value to an illicit drug operation. Large volumes of the narcotic came into many British ports and made their way into the dense populations of London. The quality of "the product" needed to be scrupulously tested for purity, and such testing required the talents of a highly skilled chemist. Michaels was thus conveniently employed. His estimable skills – skills that would have produced a very fine physician – were used to precisely distinguish product that was "pure" from product that had been adulterated with agents designed to add weight and volume to the precious commodity.

Michaels lived and worked in the shadows of a criminal enterprise, toward the defeat of which, English law had struggled for decades. London's Custom House, working with Scotland Yard, would dismantle the illegal operations of one location, and the trade would open for business in another. It was true that Michaels was heavily addicted to the drug, but in spite of his use, he was acquainted with portions of the business beyond his role as chemist. He was arrested and charged with aiding and abetting the sale of illicit compounds. Scotland Yard hoped to use him as an informant against the high-level persons who brokered international sales, transport, and wholesale distribution of the drug. The evidence that Michaels could provide might well allow for significant interdiction. However, when solitary imprisonment did not set him "singing" against his employers, Lestrade was beside himself as how to proceed.

It was at this point that Holmes's services were requested by the Custom House Commissioner. Holmes suggested he be permitted to share a cell with Michaels in the character of an aging, drunken, sot. After two days as cellmates and the calculated prodding of the detective *incognito,* Michaels remained silent. With no reasonable prospect of success remaining, Holmes was removed from the cell, and the prisoner was left alone to contemplate his deteriorating circumstances. When he was finally told of his impending court date, he became agitated to the point of illness. The police surgeon, Dr. Ackles, was called in, but Michaels demanded that Dr. John Watson be produced to examine him. As a matter of procedure, such demands by a prisoner are immediately dismissed out of hand, yet the lingering hope that evidence could be elicited prompted Lestrade to invite me personally. Michaels's choosing me as his physician had foundation in our youthful association but was essentially a fortuitous stroke of luck for the Yard. I arrived, and Holmes – in character – was hastily installed in the adjoining cell to bear witness to what Michels might possibly say to his old school chum. Unfortunately, aside from Michaels's request for me to take possession of his anatomy textbook, the jailhouse intervention did not bear evidentiary fruit. Holmes expectoration and vile swearing at me were, as he explained, the personal flourishes he employed to maintain the credibility of his assumed character as among his cutthroat cellmates.

By the time he had completed relating to me the details of this troubling narrative, Holmes had become strangely subdued and confidential.

"Forgive me, Watson," Holmes said almost sadly, "but as I am sure you know, I must admit to some experience in the realm of narcotic use and its distinctive allure... but for a man to surrender his life work, his free will, and his physical liberty to the transient pleasures of a narcotic, is a desperate and dangerous choice. It is that overreaching danger that has kept him from implicating any of his superiors in the trade. Without his evidence, I suspect my efforts in this matter have come to an unprofitable end. And as for your chum, he is caught in a trap from which I fear there is no reasonable opportunity for escape."

"Perhaps that is true, Holmes. Perhaps he is beyond redemption," I admitted reluctantly, "yet he may still be capable of assisting others with theirs. I would like to speak with him again. Now that I have a full picture of his involvement, I believe he may confide in his old schoolmate and offer me at least some scraps of information that might tend to some small reduction of this poisonous scourge."

Holmes stood silent for a moment, then turned to me with an expressive look of pathos I was sure I had never before seen upon him. "The people manipulating this industry are a murderous lot, my dear friend. Your continued involvement in the matter, were it discovered, may place your life and limb at considerable risk. You should know that at this level of criminal enterprise, retaliation for interference with 'business' – even the mere appearance of interference – is swift and lethal. You have a career and a family to consider."

"I only wish to speak with him," I rejoined, defensively, "and I would be safely within the security of his prison cell. My safety could hardly be compromised under such circumstances." Holmes did not appear convinced by my argument, and he seemed on the verge of telling me so when I cut him rather short. "I am a doctor, Holmes. My 'career' consists chiefly in preserving and maintaining human life. What sort of physician would not instinctively snatch away a bottle of poison from the hand of a patient? In good conscience, how can I possibly turn away from this?"

Holmes expression was sobering. "I have offered you my professional cautions and forebodings, Watson, but cautions and forebodings have little power over the human heart when it is moved to accomplish what it perceives as 'the good.' If you will proceed in this, my friend, proceed warily." I walked him to the office foyer, and he lifted the volume of Gray's *Anatomy* from the small table. It was certain that, at his leisure, Holmes would inspect the book with greater circumspection than the rather cursory review undertaken by Lestrade. He placed the Gray securely under his arm and stepped out toward the street.

The scene of the underground tunnels of holding cells at Scotland Yard had not changed. The drear, the odors, and the palpable desperation hung suspended in the fetid air. A uniformed officer turned key in lock and swung back the iron for me to enter. Michaels was slung upon his cot in a fetal position, no doubt suffering from the debilitation of withdrawal from his drug. I had not anticipated that his presence of mind might not be sufficiently lucid for reasonable conversation. When I gently called him by name, he swung slowly around toward me and fixed his bloodshot eyes generally upon the space where I was standing. After some moments, when he realized who I was, he seemed to rally and asked hurriedly if I had taken possession of the book from his flat. I affirmed that I had the volume, and he seemed relieved. He sat up and collected himself somewhat.

"My hearing is scheduled for tomorrow morning," he muttered. "The barrister that has been assigned to me is confident that I will be released soon thereafter. 'Released' indeed. I am told the crown's evidence against me will be shown to be 'insufficient,'" and he laughed bitterly until a spasm of coughing caught him up short.

It was at this time I realized I did not possess any interrogation skills and knew not at all how to begin. It must have sounded childishly simple, but I looked at him intently and asked, "Is there anything you want to tell me? Might you let me help you in some way or other?"

His shoulders slumped, he looked down at the floor of the cell and shook his head in the negative.

Somehow, I knew then that his silence would not relent. The secrets he possessed about the London drug trade would never be revealed. He would take them to his grave, and if his intimation was correct, that grave would be coming for him not too far along. The thought of that – of his wasted life and squandered talents – suddenly angered me.

"Why did you want to see me, then," I asked in a raised voice. "You asked for me by name – why ever did you do such a thing? You and I are no relation, we were hardly close chums at school, you were the dandy of the class, and I was the sheltered book worm. What could ever have possessed you to call for me from your jail cell? You must have wanted something! Tell me, what is it...what was it?" I stood there flustered by his silence, and by his fatality, and by his refusal to explain what part I played in his ruined misspent life.

He stared up at me thoughtfully and a smile slowly came across his face. "You took the anatomy award," he said, as though those words would make all things clear to me. "I had taken almost every other award at university, but you took the anatomy honors. I always admired that about you. You never could have known, but I wanted to be more like you and less like me, because you were settled and focused, and I was ever scattered and searching – searching for things our books and studying could never give me. You became what I could never have become. I admire you, Dr. Watson."

I muttered some exclamation of denial to these commendations of his.

"Do not mistake me – I am no flatterer," he said sharply. "Is it really so very strange that I wanted to meet with you again, that I wanted you to have my copy of Gray's? That book is all I have ... to offer you... to offer anyone. I am undone," he said in a whisper, and fell back on his cot with his face to the wall.

"I am sure I do not know what to say to all this," I replied in a stammer. "You need not throw it all up, Michaels. There is still time to turn about from this sordid business and start anew, brush aside the shadows and step into the light." When it became clear I could not coax another word from the man, I summoned the guard and made my way out of the station. It is a tragic thing to see a man sell his soul, but quite another tragedy to see him fritter it away one small piece at a time.

Three days passed during which period I had written to Lestrade more than once requesting a police patrol be assigned to protect Michaels from the death he had predicted would befall him soon after his release. My pleas were fruitless. The official response was consistently dismissive: Scotland Yard does not provide protective services for previously incarcerated persons. On its face, and in my heart, I knew this was not an unreasonable policy. Holmes had sent me word asking that I visit him, but I had neglected my patients of late and needed to restore the hours I had spent busying and brooding over the Michaels' affair. Days later, when I was finally able to bring myself around to Baker Street, Holmes greeted me with a pitying look, uncertain whether I had read the two-inch *Times* column on the fourth page recounting the suspected drug-related death of one Geoffrey Walton Michaels.

"Have you seen the *Times?*" he asked with as much sensitivity as he could muster.

"Yes," I replied plaintively. "I do not know why his passing should affect me so. His end was the end of many who descend into the world of narcotic use. I have seen it often and have tried to treat it often. Nevertheless, when you know the fellow – when you have laughed with him and broke bread with him – it is a passing not so easy to dismiss. I fear that the 'clinical disposition' that doctors are supposed to cultivate has quite abandoned me, Holmes," I said sadly.

It took me no longer than a few moments to realize that Holmes was in a mood strangely unique to his usual dispositions. He was a man so often absorbed by his own thoughts, that to see him so seriously considerate of mine, was a phenomenon for which I was hardly prepared. Apparently, my distress upon the death of Michaels was affecting me to a greater extent than I knew myself. Holmes was being genuinely solicitous. He saw to my being comfortably seated, to Mrs. Hudson bringing in tea, and to his sitting by quietly and focusing upon my ramblings with an attention uncharacteristic of the desultory indifference of Sherlock Holmes. All this was a welcome reminder that Holmes, the calculating machine of deductive observation and the coldly intuitive mastermind, was one who knew when and how to comfort a friend. This was a trait in him so seldom expressed, that its appearance was so much the more valued.

After a moment or two of tea and talk, Holmes rose, stepped to the sideboard, and retrieved the copy of Gray's *Anatomy* that I had secured from Michaels's flat and that Holmes had borrowed from me several days earlier. He carried it over to the divan and reseated himself, cradling the volume in his hands and turning the pages indiscriminately.

"What is it precisely that Michaels told you about this book, Watson?" Holmes asked finally.

"Very little, to be honest, Holmes. He made quite a stir about my getting hold of it first off. Then later, when I revisited him, he said it was the only thing he had to offer me, ... and then he said something rather strange. He said the book was all that he had, 'to offer anyone.' It struck me as an odd remark, but then, he was distraught and in a depressed state of mind. Being incarcerated must have a way of jumbling the things a man may think and say.

"As you were kind enough to lend me his text, Watson, I took the liberty of turning through the pages, and in the process, I made a rather interesting discovery." Holmes had turned to the approximate center of the volume, opened it fully, and turned the book around to face me, exposing the right and left pages fully to my view. The printing on the pages had been either bleached or painted over, and a very small, very neat handwriting resembling mathematical or chemical symbols covered the space where the original printing had once appeared.

I squinted at the rows and columns of the hand-drawn figures for a moment, then looked at Holmes perplexed. I reached over, lifted the book from him, and began leafing through the sheets. Originally, the volume contained well over one thousand pages of anatomical science studies. Michaels's copy obliterated the printed ink on perhaps 100 of the center pages and they had been rewritten upon in a clean, concentrated handwritten script. Clearly these pages were notes of chemical equations, the results of chemical missteps and re-calculations, with marginal notes of a complex character, all of which were clearly legible and orderly.

"I am afraid I do not understand, Holmes," I remarked confusedly. "This is Michaels's book, and so I assume these are his notes, but what are they, and why would he have inserted them into a printed text?"

"As for your first question, Watson, my science studies are admittedly no match for your own, but I have reviewed these pages carefully and at length," Holmes explained in his familiar tone of the enlightened schoolmaster. "The chemical formulas and calculations here speak to the building of a compound that might be described by the layman as a 'pain reducing pill.' If the chemistry is sound, these notes give evidence that science may be on the threshold of producing a simple pharmaceutical that would alleviate a significant portion of human distress. The work here is not complete, but it travels far enough to clear much of the way for a landmark in medical advance. It seems your school chum was more than he appeared to be."

"As for your second question, my friend, there remains only speculation – and I despise speculation. It is an inconclusive operation of the mind that I conscientiously avoid. However, for your sake and under these unusual circumstances, it is speculation in which I will indulge, and it is simply this: Michaels was a ruined man with a conscience wracked by the guilt of knowing what he might have become had he not succumbed to the lure of narcotic pleasure. In his moments of lucidity, he turned this guilt into a palpable creative force. No doubt he was a man of considerable scientific intellect. I believe he secreted his formulations onto the bleached pages of a highly regarded textbook in the belief that someday someone would turn through those renowned pages and discover his work. A mere notebook or journal might easily have been discarded or tossed aside by any unsuspecting uninformed person. When he was taken into custody and faced with the reality of his impending death at the hands of his criminal cohort, he wanted a more immediate assurance that his work would be seen and understood. You, my dear Watson, with your steadfast morals and inherent loyalty to an old school chum, represented that assurance."

I sat quietly for several moments while the weight of what Holmes had expounded upon settled in my heart and mind. The brightness of Michaels's youthful exuberance, and the dark nature of his wasteful end crowded together suddenly in my thoughts. What are we to make of such men as Michaels? What can any man expect when all his evil and all his good are heaped upon the scales in the final judgement?

Holmes could see that I was lost in troubling thoughts. His voice softened when he turned to speak to me. "I have done some small research into this science of your chum, Watson. It seems that there is a scientist who is presently engaged in very similar work. Felix Hoffmann is employed by a pharmaceutical company in Barmen, Germany. He is working on various combinations of *acetyl* and *spiraea*. If his research succeeds, the compound is to be referred to as 'aspirin.' Your friend's work, hidden in the pages of his old anatomy textbook, may be invaluable to this Hoffman fellow."

Holmes lifted the heavy text and his voice remained subdued. "Michael's notes in this book may prove to be the redemption you had hoped for him, Watson. With your approval," he said quietly, "I will write an explanatory letter and prepare the volume for special delivery to the German Republic."

The Adventure of the Visiting Soprano

My associations with the celebrated London detective, Mr. Sherlock Holmes, were not ever as frequent as they may have seemed to those familiar with the short narratives I have composed about Holmes's criminal investigations. Readers of those accounts may very well assume that I spent a good deal of my time assisting Holmes in matters of criminal justice. If truth be told, I am first and foremost a physician. I grant that my practice was not one of London's most flourishing medical enterprises, but the practice of medicine is my profession; it is what my training prepared me for, and what my personal inclination has drawn me towards these 20 years. Assisting Holmes in his criminal inquiries and memorializing the details of select criminal episodes are my avocations, not my profession. Nevertheless, I am not displeased to have practical experience in both domains. I have often had reason to apply my medical skills in the criminal realm, and I am sorry to admit that I have too often glimpsed elements of criminality in the medical field. Crime and medicine may not be common bedfellows, but neither are they necessarily antithetical, a theme that I have discussed briefly in "The Case of the Tainted Will." It seems to me that medicine seeks to preserve human life while crime either manipulates people's instinct to cling to life or disregards it altogether. The distinctions between the two are therefore sharp, but their intersections are not as infrequent as might be thought.

It is precisely these observations that bring to mind a story that began to unfold during the mid-summer season two years past. The upcoming weather promised to be quite delightful, and so I had taken a short and much-deserved holiday. I reserved rooms at one of those highly regarded shoreline resorts so much admired by its guests that many of them tend most zealously to keep the location of the retreat a strict secret from the world at large. I have actually spoken with fellow vacationers who have scolded me for revealing the name of the haven in public for fear it will adulterate the spot and cause marauding hordes from the cities to render it thereafter uninhabitable. It is this degree of human zeal in matters that are otherwise utter foolishness that has led me on occasion to a questionable judgment of my fellowman.

In any event, I was lounging one oppressively warm afternoon on the terrace of the not-to-be-named hideaway, and I happened to fall into conversation with a fellow physician. The weather would have been unbearable but for the large table umbrella shielding us from the sun, and the intermittent sea breeze wafting up from the rocky shoreline. When the conversation finally strayed from the discomforts of the weather, the subject of our shared profession was the unavoidable alternative. His name was Jedson. He was an administrator at Saint John's Hospital in Leichester, and precisely the type of fellow I hope to avoid, but invariably encounter, on holiday. After hearing what seemed an interminable discussion of the burdensome responsibilities of his post, and the irremediable laxity of his staff, he launched quite predictably into a torrent of self-adulation. While I sat listening politely, I could not help but think how I so much preferred the quiet, often silent musing and brooding times spent with my friend, Sherlock Holmes. Holmes's social manners may have been abhorrent and his personal habits difficult to endure, but the simple pleasure of his company was a thing worthy of special appreciation.

My holiday tablemate spoke on incessantly, and I was rapidly approaching the point of fabricating some pressing engagement on the croquet green, that might excuse me from having to further endure his harangue, when he quite unexpectedly took up a subject that vaguely promised to be of interest.

It seemed that recently, one of the aging widowers on the geriatric ward at St. John's had begun a courtship, became engaged while in hospital, and was actually married on the ward while reclined in his sick bed. This unique marital union was the talk of every member of the staff. Their

97

opinions on the matter were evenly divided between a warm support for the romance of an aging love affair, and a cooler objection to the advantage being taken by a younger woman of a lonely and seriously ill older man. The gentleman in the connection was conspicuously wealthy, and his family – as small and distant as it was – protested the match vehemently.

When my fellow-healer saw that my interest had been somewhat aroused by the narrative, he began to launch into further particulars with no less enthusiasm than the most common back-street gossip. He warmed to the story with a leering ardor that seemed somehow inappropriate for a professional man who held such an elevated position of responsibility. Is it not an intriguing dichotomy that our public selves and private selves can be so distinctly different? I believe it was a French writer who explained that when we wear one face to the world and another to ourselves, we often become confused as to which we are. My storyteller was continuing his tale of the seemingly mismatched spouses, and my attention slowly refocused on his seamy narrative.

"The woman," he said with a sly smile, "was strikingly attractive, and very barely beyond the blush of her youth. She had begun visiting her 'gentleman,' as she referred to him, quite by accident when the person she had originally planned to visit in hospital had apparently been discharged. Discharged indeed," he exclaimed with a wink and a grin. "The actual identity of this alleged 'discharged patient' was never discovered. Come now," he exclaimed to me in a confidential tone, "she had learned of a rich old codger in hospital, came specifically to see him, claimed the false pretense of a charitable visitation, struck up a conversation with this Wrenkle fellow, and plied him with her estimable charms. Three weeks later, the old boy had taken her to wive. Oh my stars, 'what a tangled web we weave,' Doctor" he said laughing. "Personally old chap, I think his entanglement with her served him right. She must have taken the fellow for tens of thousands of pounds."

"What do you mean, 'taken the fellow?'" I asked casually. "Did she raid his accounts or ruin his business interests?"

"Gracious no, my good man! Nothing as scurrilous as that. He simply died... died within a fortnight, two weeks to the day after he was released from St. John's, and she inherited every shilling he possessed. The staff knew Wrenkle would not see Michaelmas, and it is beyond cavil that his darling bride knew it as well. No doubt it was a dastardly plot, but no laws were broken. Some might say it was a pretty profit for a few hours researching the old boy's riches, and a few weeks of 'visiting hours.' It was generally common knowledge on the wards that she was winding him about her little finger, but of course, the hospital could not intervene. Come evenings, before visitors' hours ended, she would sing to him with a voice like an angel. The fluid notes would float down the hospital hallways like soft summer breezes. Not a patient or a staff member ever lodged a single complaint of her singing. Hers was always a compelling performance. If she was not professionally trained, I am a fishmonger."

"Did his family move against her in the probate court?" I inquired. "Perhaps she had unduly influenced the old boy or had overborne his discretion. Doubts might have been cast upon the estate."

"What manner of doctor are you, old man? Is St. Greg's a lonely-hearts club?" he asked sarcastically. "You must know that once a patient is discharged from hospital, his life and times are his own and of no further consequence to the institution... and thank a gracious God for that. I am no nursemaid to some lonely old fool. Good riddance, I say."

The simple story of an 'old fool' – a story that had stirred in me little more than a mild interest – had grown upon me considerably. Something in the unfolding elements of Jedson's little chronicle sparked dormant memories of the brand of woman he described: her cunning, her calculation, her beauty, her careful skirting along the edges of the law, her manipulation of men, and her voice. Inadvertently, this hospital administrator, sipping a cool drink on the veranda of a remote coastal retreat, had recalled the pieces of a troubling picture to my mind, and the picture was of the beauty and dark talents of Irene Adler. Dr. Jedson's brief portraiture of the newlywed Mrs. Wrenkle brought the image of Adler clearly before my mind's eye. I knew that "the woman" - as Holmes invariably referred to Adler - was long dead, but the memories of her provocations and the insidious threat to undermine the planned marriage of the King of Bohemia were sufficiently robust to keep her image vividly alive. The very thought that there were other members of the female sex as insidious as she, roaming about provoking chaos and dissolution, unsettled me. The more remote possibility that Adler had only feigned her death and had reappeared under an assumed name was thoroughly disarming. I therefore lifted my whiskey and soda and took a long pull at the glass before I nervously posed my next question to Jedson.

"Did you know her by her maiden name, or only as Mrs. Wrenkle," I asked as casually as I could, though being casual was hardly possible.

Jedson looked over at me indifferently to respond with beverage in hand. "Before the marriage, she was required to sign in at hospital as a visitor," he said languidly. "Ordinarily, I would retain no recollection of incidentals as mundane as visitor sign-ins, but she was such a sensation among the staff, her name was constantly being bandied about. As I recall," he mused, "the name was... Morris, or Morton... no it was Meriden, yes... Theresa Meriden.

I sat back in the sagging wicker chair able to breathe again, knowing it was not Adler. However, I could not put aside completely the thoughts of Adler that rattled about in my mind. The woman Jedson described resembled her in too many disturbing ways. The late Irene Adler was the manipulative influencer at the center of a case that Holmes and I had been involved in years before. The charms, the beauty, and the voice of Theresa Meriden all seemed the very same parts of the enchanting and thoroughly beguiling Adler who had set her wits against those of London's most brilliant detective... and had won. For Holmes, it was a loss from which he never fully recovered. He could not allow the Adler case details to dim and dissolve into obscurity. For him, those details remained painful reminders of a defeat. Holmes kept the loss and the memory of Irene Adler 'close to the vest.' The detective had very honorably admitted to having fallen out on the wrong side of three other case matters in his career, but the disappointment of the Adler case was a prickling thorn stuck in the paw of this lion. Adler's death was a disagreeable fact that deprived Holmes of ever enjoying the dark pleasures of visiting retribution upon a deserving opponent.

Jedson saw that my mind had wandered to some place well aside from the details of his story. I tried not to appear unsettled. If Holmes were there, he would have read my trailing thoughts in an instant. Of course, I did not share my conjectures regarding Adler with Jedson. It would seem to him a fantastic leap of improbability, and so it was. Nevertheless, my mind and memory were wandering about and trying to force together puzzle pieces that did not align. If it were true that the name Theresa Meriden was merely an alias, then was it not at least possible that Adler, long thought dead, could be alive and well? Surely, my mind was miscarrying. Though it may have been a thing possible, it was most assuredly improbable. Holmes always propounded that probabilities were to be depended upon, and possibilities summarily dismissed.

The newlywed Theresa Meriden-Wrengle may have had some of the character trappings of Irene Adler, but then many members of our species are schooled in deception. A calculating woman may use her natural beauty aggressively to her own aggrandizement. She may assume names meant to deceive or disparage others. She could approach a vulnerable man and use her wiles to draw him to herself in the guise of romantic interest. What Mrs. Wrengle was, and what she purported to be, might well have been two images that were worlds apart.

I repaired to my bungalow, sifted through the available data as Holmes would have me do, and concluded that possibilities cannot be transformed into probabilities upon whim. That Theresa Wrengle was a controlling and manipulating deceiver was a distinct possibility but, based upon the data and evidence provided in the narrative of Dr. Jedson, it was a possibility that had not been elevated to the status of the probable. I wondered whether Holmes would have agreed with my reasoning.

Two days later I returned to London and spent a good deal of time considering whether to acquaint Holmes with the details of the Wrengle marriage in Leichester, and its reminiscence of the Irene Adler case . I knew that even a passing reference to "the woman," as Holmes invariably referred to Adler, might stir within him shards of disagreeable memories. That was not a current I was anxious to swirl into motion against my friend. Should I reveal that this Leichester bride reminded me of Adler herself, or should I keep every detail of the Wrengle marriage entirely hushed and untold? If I spoke of the Wrengle marriage to any extent, the connection to Adler would be unavoidable and I would be opening an old wound. If I avoided discussion of the matter altogether, I might be withholding the story of a woman who was as manipulative and calculating as Irene Adler had been - a story in which the detective might well have taken a significant professional interest. I realized that concealing from Holmes everything I had heard about the hospital marriage in Leichester was hardly a viable option. Five minutes in his presence would be sufficient time for him to deduce my unease, and the plot to conceal it from him would hopelessly unravel.

What was then to be done? The only alternative was to absent myself from him for a period long enough for me to decide the proper course of action. I realized this was only a short-term solution, but it was the only solution my sluggish conscience could conceive. I therefore resolved to keep mum with Holmes on both topics: the amusing story of an apparently contrived marriage in a Leichester hospital, and the appearance of a woman whose activities were strangely emblematic of Irene Adler's *modus operandi*. The two incidents were inextricably merged I knew, and the decision to either reveal or conceal was my Gordian knot.

I resumed the normal duties at my medical office and at St. Gregory's. Two months' time had passed before I hardly thought two weeks had. Patients were cared for, rounds at the hospital were completed, domestic obligations were attended to, and aside from the seashore's beastly heat, the details of my recent holiday began to fade into somewhat pleasant memories. Try as I may, however, the very thought that a clever counterpart of Irene Adler might be lurking about, weaving some new web of deception, was an almost omnipresent weight upon me. This weight, increased by my sense of guilt for not having yet revealed to Holmes my intimations regarding the matter, was cause for a lingering uneasiness in me. I had never before purposefully withheld information from Holmes, especially not information touching upon any investigation we had worked upon. Nonetheless, I held fast to my decision not to divulge what were only my suspicions and silently endured my gnawing anxiety.

I had neither seen nor spoken to Holmes for many weeks. It was early evening of a Thursday in late August, and I was at St. Gregory's somewhat later than usual, having had a long consult with a colleague on a difficult case of respiratory infection. The consulting physician and I were chatting casually with the hospital chief-of-staff when suddenly the soft, gentle notes of a woman's voice in song could be heard moving faintly through the corridors. The bittersweet sadness of the melody echoed gently down the hallways. The song was a wildly popular one. It was *"Musetta's Waltz"* from the new opera, *La Boheme* by the Italian composer, Puccini. The lyrics were in choice Italian, but even with words foreign to the English ear, the sheer emotion of the melody struck at the heart. For weeks it seemed that everywhere a piano sat, the tune was being played, and whenever accompanying words and melody ushered from the voice of a worthy artist, every listener was enthralled. For a moment, even I was caught up in the melancholy cadence of the fretful song.

When my moment of reverie finally passed, and I fitfully regained my practical senses, my first thought went like a shot to Theresa Meriden Wrangle, and her cunning marriage at St. John's Hospital in Leichester. Was she also a trained operatic singer as Adler had been? If my poor judgment were of any value, the voice singing at that moment was a soprano of the highest order. Adler was a contralto. I finally excused myself from my colleagues on the grounds of some business or other and moved anxiously toward the sound... but not soon enough. By the time I had covered but a few steps, the faint singing stopped.

I made my way upstairs from whence the song was heard and found myself on the geriatric ward. My hasty inquiries to staff revealed that the singer had left hospital. The ward nurse was voluble in her account of the matter. The song had poured forth from the private room of an elderly gentleman, Senor Giacomo Despranos, a wealthy Spanish-born businessman. The patient, who was seriously ill, was a great favorite with the staff. It seems he was a kind old fellow, and having never married, he had no children and few visitors. How fortunate for him, the staff all agreed, that he had recently made the acquaintance of a lovely young female visitor quite by chance, and they had formed a fast friendship in only a few short weeks. These unexpected developments gave fortification to the thin strands of my lurking suspicions. It was the alluring song of this visitor that ended finally my hesitating deliberation. For me, the line had been crossed from the possible to the probable.

I dashed off a message to Holmes asking that he see me without delay. He sent back word that I should come to him at my very earliest convenience to confer with him on a matter that was of pressing concern to an important client. I was prepared to tell him everything I had learned regarding the appearance in no less than two British hospitals of a criminal-minded woman cut from the cloth of an Irene Adler. I was further prepared to accept whatever recrimination he may have thought the circumstances of my silence might have deserved. My hesitations may well have given an unscrupulous Mrs. Meriden-Wrengle the chance to arrange yet another marriage of opportunity upon yet another unwell, unsuspecting elderly gentleman. My months of inaction shamed me. The carriage ride to Baker Street and the walk up the stairs to my old lodgings were accomplished with a heavy heart. Holmes was a friend, and I feared I had done him an injustice by not only concealing matters indicating latent criminal activity but possibly enabling the criminal herself in the commission of her next conquest.

I entered the flat and Holmes and I exchanged greetings as any two friends might who had had not seen one another for a time longer than that to which they were accustomed. Before I could launch into the stories of my previous suspicions and present fears regarding Theresa Meriden-Wrangle, Holmes asked me to seat myself comfortably, drew up a chair beside me, and began to speak in tones that, unlike his usual passionless demeanor, were almost apologetic in their tenor. "I must make a confession to you, my friend," he said slowly, "and the details of it touch upon matters of our mutual and incommutable trust."

This was not the first time that Holmes had uttered words which utterly confounded me, but the irony of his suggesting that he needed to make a confession to me for something he had done, was astonishing. I knew that it was my confession that needed to be offered and heard, not his. However, under the circumstances, I thought it best to sit quietly, contain my madding confusion, and listen to whatever guilty burden he needed to dislodge.

He leaned forward in his chair and rested his elbows on his knees before he began to speak. "Several months ago, I was contacted by a very wealthy and very powerful European family that was deeply concerned that an aging member of their brood presently residing in London might be susceptible to a plot of extortion or fraudulent deception. This family member's advancing age, failing health, and thoroughly trusting and naive nature, gave them cause to foresee that an unscrupulous person or business competitor might influence him to the family's detriment. It is a matter, my dear Watson, precisely upon which your discreet involvement would be invaluable. My preliminary research, and a nagging premonition such as I would much have preferred to disregard, suggested the presence of an old female nemesis. Some years ago, you may recall there were claims of her untimely death. Were 'the woman' still alive, her movements under an assumed name may have afforded her enlarged opportunities for mischief. I see you are almost aghast. Yes, Watson," Holmes said solemnly, "I speak of 'the woman,' Irene Adler Norton.

"Let me say foremost, that my initial research conclusively determined that all certifications of Adler's death were unquestionably *bona fide*. When that fact was established, I contacted my client, the Despranos family of Madrid to explain that a broader, far-reaching review of potential suspects needed to be undertaken. They immediately granted me *carte blanche* in the matter. These many months I have maintained absolute secrecy at the family's insistence.

"It is my not having shared this confidence with you, my friend, that has concerned me to distraction these several passing months. You should know, however, that I have recently wired my clients to inform them that my trusted associate must be brought onto the case. I regret not having done so earlier, and it is for this lapse in discretion that you have my sincere apologies, doctor."

Holmes leaned back and reached for his pipe, an interruption that promised an opportunity for me to acquaint him with my suspicions from the incident at St. John's in Leichester, but before I could begin, he tossed the empty Meerschaum back onto the littered tabletop and quickly resumed his oration.

"As is not uncommon at the onset of many of our cases, Watson, a crime has yet to be committed. Our employment here is in the hope of prevention rather than the apprehension associated with a post-crime circumstance. My three threshold inquiries in the matter were straightforward: first, who is most likely to succeed in exerting irresistible influence over rich, elderly, unmarried men in seriously poor health? With all reasonable deference to the incomparable qualities of the female sex, the irrefutable answer is, 'a woman.' The second interrogative followed quite logically: if a woman were so disposed to formulate marital connections for personal gain how might she find vulnerable men suited to her designs? The obvious answer is, in hospital. The third and final query was most crucial: how can the identity of a woman so inclined be discovered. The answer to this question was not easily achieved. It required intense and expansive research into hospital records and marriage records and most especially into those circumstances where, as they occasionally do, these two otherwise disparate files of data intersect. I have no doubt, Watson, that the ruthlessness of the feminine characteristics in this matter must have brought to your mind the name of an old adversary.

"Irene Adler?" I opined innocently.

"Precisely," Holmes rejoined. "As I am sure you recall, Adler was the instigator behind the plot threatening to wreak havoc on the marriage of King Wilhelm of Bohemia, a tale I believe you selected to chronicle from among our investigative endeavors. My very first determination several months ago was to assure myself that the account of Adler's death was not fabricated. When her demise was rendered certain, I initiated thoroughly concurrent probes through the records of London hospitals via several teams of researchers seeking that intersection of in-hospital marriage of geriatric men to younger women." Holmes reclined slowly into the back of his chair as if to punctuate his continuing comments. "Persons seeking to conceal themselves and their activities from public scrutiny have certain advantages, Watson. Fortunately, recordkeeping is an exact science. We should thank God for the firmness and stolid natures of our British civil servants who keep British records with the same precision of our finest timepieces. They are unwavering and relentless. The enterprise of uncovering these unique marital connections was monumental, and it was one undertaken at no small expenditure in time or money, but eventually, success was achieved.

"Several hospital marriages were recorded, but only a handful of these involved spouses of significantly different ages, and of those, even fewer than a handful were shown to have occurred in instances where the male patient was a fellow of significant financial means. One union in particular featured a woman of considerable youth wed to an older, well-heeled gentleman whose very life was dangling precipitously. The demise of the gentleman occurred less than a fortnight from the very time of the bedside ceremony. Some little further review revealed that the grieving widow shortly thereafter initiated extensive travel to the major cities of the Continent, particularly to the luxury hotels of those major cities. Her style of living was sumptuous and elaborate.

"Eventually, those standards began to show a decided reduction in luxury, until finally, her condition resembled the penurious wanderings of a woman with high taste and low means. It must be a difficult thing, Watson, for a woman who has tasted the flavors of extravagant

113

Continental life, to accept the bitterness of indigence and destitution. The looming prospects of poverty seen by an ambitious woman are sturdy encouragements to return to and perpetuate wrongdoing that promises wealth. Such a woman finds herself in desperate need of a reliable plan that will provide her with a steadying stream of disposable riches.

"For a woman with beauty and a paucity of conscience, the plan is not one troubled with complexity, Watson. It is simply this: find, woo, and wed successive sickly, elderly, and wealthy unmarried men. From this simple formula, she creates a veritable industry of wealth appropriation. The most recent iteration of the plan was employed at St. John's Hospital in Leicester where the would-be bride purposefully acquainted herself with a hospitalized elderly gentleman who was near his life's end...."

"David Wrenkle," I interjected with some small suavity. "And the woman's name is Meriden... Theresa Meriden."

"Why... yes," Holmes stammered, "but how could you possibly have..."

This was truly a unique and unforeseen *denouement* in my long association with the detective. I possessed information about a case, and Holmes was at a loss as to how

I had acquired it. This situation was almost always reversed; it was he who would possess facts, the revelation of which would astonish his faithful associate. Of course, my knowing the name of David Wrengle was not the result of some brilliant deduction, nor had I the mystical gifts of an omniscient. Facts, as Holmes was want to remind me at every turn, were almost always obvious things. The detective was surprised that I knew the name because he was completely unaware of my conversation with Dr. Jedson during my holiday. My resulting familiarity with the Wrengle marriage was mere chance. I do not admire myself for admitting it, but to some small extent, I was enjoying this rather remarkable reversal. All these considerations were in my thoughts, but I did not give voice to any of them. Rather, I looked over at the detective sheepishly.

"Forgive me, Holmes," I said, determined to conceal my little private victory, "but my knowing of the Wrengle matter in Leichester is both fortuitous and inconsequential at this juncture. Therefore, pray continue."

Holmes looked at me askance, caught himself up slowly, then resumed his narrative somewhat haltingly, I thought.

"There were two other elderly 'targets' before Theresa's connection to Wrengle in Leichester. She had followed the same formula with a gentleman from Camberly and another fellow in Charhaven Cross. Both were elderly, ill, and of some means. However, their wealth was not nearly a match for Wrengle's. Even he was not possessed of means adequate to indefinitely finance the unbridled expenses of a spendthrift prodigal wife. In but a few short months, when her accounts began to thin yet again, she took to scanning the London city hospitals in search for yet another, perhaps better-advantaged host upon whom to parasitically attach herself. This was the very situation that my Spanish clients, the Despranos, had so fearfully anticipated and had engaged me to discourage or prevent. Theresa Williams, who became Theresa Meridan, who became Theresa Wrenkle, has focused her most recent sights upon my client's patriarch, Senor Giacomo Despranos, a conspicuously wealthy importer whose family commands an international wealth that exceeds the treasuries of several crowned heads of Europe.

"As you may be aware, Watson, Giacomo Despranos is presently a patient at your own St. Gregory's Hospital," Holmes said, with a distinctly suspicious glance directed at my person. "A successful marital connection to the riches of the Despranos' family would elevate Mrs. Wrengle to circumstances providing a lifetime of obscene extravagance. If her marital bans are duly announced and her nuptial ceremony is certified, she would become an extraordinarily wealthy and internationally powerful woman."

"Holmes," I said with conviction, "I realize now that failing to inform you early on was a grave error. I became aware of the Wrengle marriage incident while on holiday early this summer and it brought with it disturbing intimations of Irene Adler. I hesitated to inform you for fear it would dredge up your unpleasant memories. I should have immediately telegraphed my suspicions to you. Yesterday, I heard a woman singing beautifully in the halls at St. Gregorys. The song issued from Despranos's room. It was the same song sung to David Wrengle at St. John's in Leichester. I should have dispatched a messenger to you posthaste. I fear my hesitations here may have done harm or paved its way."

"You have done no harm whatsoever, my friend," Holmes reassured me. "Do not give that thought the very least consideration. The new Mrs. Theresa Wrengle is a manipulative machine. It is her life's pleasure to hoodwink the male of the species. Her charms, her beauty, and her angel's voice are her weapons, and they are estimable ones indeed. That she is now upon her fourth conquest owes nothing to your hesitations. The exigent issue and the only one worthy of our collective cogitations is whether anything in the world of English common law can be done to stop her."

"'....whether anything can be done to stop her,'" I asked incredulously. "How can that be, Holmes? The woman is a fraud, a conniver, and a menace to civil order. Is there no English law against using the sacred and civil propriety of marriage as a tool to deceive spouses and deprive them of their riches? Is it not some form of homicide to premeditate the death of David Wrengle in order to relieve him of his purse? Has she not defrauded at least two English hospitals by ingratiating herself with unsuspecting wealthy patients to the point of their death or ruin? Forgive me, Holmes. You know I am not usually given to tirade, but how can she not be in violation of English law?"

"In spite of my estimable legal knowledge, Watson, I am no barrister. Nevertheless, the knowledge I do possess teaches, *nulla injuria, nullum remedium* – where there is no wrong, there is no remedy. To date, Miss Theresa has brought three men, each of their own accord, to the bonds of wedlock. In the absence of bigamy, mistake, or civil regulatory breach, each marriage was legally binding on the parties and resulted in enforceable testamentary or intestate distributions of the deceased spouse's property, both personal and real. When her duly espoused husbands died from what appeared to be medically documented difficulties, she became the surviving spouse. Currently, she is courting Despranos, and if she marries him, she becomes heir to his fortune. She may be a contemptible, odious, and loathsome creature in the plannings and arrangements of her various marital enterprises, but under current British law, she is not a criminal."

"Can we do nothing then, Holmes," I asked desperately. The woman has perpetrated fraud, deceptively appropriated funds, and she may very well be doing a good deal more of the same almost as we speak."

Holmes reached again for the large hook-stemmed meerschaum. He loaded it this time with the dark-flaked Cavendish that so often filled the room with impenetrable clouds of its odorous fog. I knew he had heard my last remark. His thoughts were churning away within him. His mind, I knew, was sifting through the disappointing limitations of the law, and the much more satisfying possibilities available when justice found its own path. When he spoke, I was sure he had conceived an appropriate plan, but its elements were as unknown to me as the headlines of tomorrow's *London Times*.

"Watson, I must telegraph my clients in Madrid and tell them that their patriarch is in danger of being compromised, and I must wait for their reply. If their answer is as I expect, we need to move forward on the matter with all possible speed. Tell me, doctor, is it possible that using your influence at St. Gregory's, you might arrange for me to visit with Senor Despranos at a time during which visitors are not permitted to see patients? I cannot risk interrupting or being interrupted by Theresa."

"Yes," I replied confidently, "I am sure that can be arranged." I did not inquire into the intended purposes of my friend's designs. My years of association with Holmes had taught me that if the plan were his, the plan was sound. I left Baker Street confident that Holmes had engineered a solution that would bring a timely end to the recklessness and aberrant behaviors of Theresa Meriden-Wrengle.

Visiting hours at St. Gregory's had come to an end. The nurses on duty in the geriatric wing informed me that Mrs. Wrengle had in fact visited Senor Despranos's private room earlier in the day and had sung a beautiful aria to him, much to the delight of the staff. Were I on call at the time, I would have been greatly tempted to visit the wing and glimpse a woman as heartless and selfishly self-possessed as Theresa Wrengle must be to live and thrive as she did. I wondered if any of the timeless, softly enduring qualities of the female sex resided in her. Did she ever possess that brand of selfless love for hearth, home, and children that clings to womankind like a warm cloak? Was her heart animated more by what she could give others than what she might have gained for the giving? Could she love someone, and labor for them, and worry over them, and nurse them, and sacrifice everything for them while knowing they might well sacrifice nothing for her? For those are the qualities of woman. From what was known of Theresa Wrengle from her recent histories, the question was not what kind of woman she was, but rather whether she deserved to be referred to as a woman at all.

Holmes had sent me a message asking that we meet inconspicuously in the hospital lobby, and he arrived promptly at the specified hour. It was late in the day and so the lobby was slowly discharging its usual crowds of staff, visitors, and collaterals as Holmes and I moved to a quiet corner to confer.

"The communication with the Despranos family proceeded as I had hoped," he said with assurance. "Now, all that remains is that our elderly gentleman be advised and brought to an understanding of his precarious circumstances. Lonely men are not often the finest examples of sound reasoning when the topic is the attentions they receive from younger attractive women. Let us hope he is of a receptive nature, Watson."

We made our way through the now quiet halls to the private room of Giacomo Maria Santiago Despranos. I approached the bedside and greeted the patient warmly in my role as one of the hospital physicians. Holmes stood quietly at the foot of the bed. I could not imagine how the detective would ever manage a situation as delicate and awkward as having to tell a man that the woman who had expressed an interest in him is a deceitful shameless fraud bent upon his utter ruin. Holmes, however, stepped up fearlessly to the bedside, and began without the slightest hesitancy.

"Good evening, Senor Despranos. My name is Sherlock Holmes. I am an investigative detective and a close associate and friend of Doctor Watson. I have been engaged by members of your family, sir, to prevent any unscrupulous persons from taking undue advantage of you during this hopefully short period of your poor health." Holmes paused here, no doubt to assess whether the patient was capable of understanding what had been said to him.

Despranos was in a well-appointed private room and was reclining in the standard issue hospital bed. His arms were lying at his sides, and he was sitting in an upright position by the aid of several pillows gathered at the head of the bed for that purpose. He held his head straight and looked from one to the other of his visitors as he was addressed by them. His facial expression was alert, his eyes were clear, but the unnatural thinness of his frame and the rather pale coloring of his skin, marked him as a man suffering from a serious illness. When he spoke, there were heavy traces of an Iberian accent, and while his voice was distinct, it was evident that speaking required him to exert a concentrated effort.

"Forgive me for come to the point swiftly, Mr. Holmes, but I believe you wish to speak with me for the concern of Theresa Wrengle..., am I correct?"

"Yes," Holmes replied simply.

"Theresa is the lovely creature and the very talented soprano. She has been visiting me and showering me with much compliment," he said dryly and smiled. "The voice she sings for me is true invaluable the gift of God. Many years in London I am, Mr. Holmes. My family is worried that I can make the mistake with this woman. Perhaps they have forgotten some things good about Giacomo. I love my family. Family is the only love, Mr. Holmes. Theresa is the fun and the beauty, but not the love. She makes me to smile, but I see in her heart there is no the smiling, no the laughing. She is the beautiful singing bird, but she is also yes some of the bird of prey. Tell me what my family desires to me – tell me of what you desire, Mr. Holmes, and I will comply it. Where there is together the beautiful young woman and the sick old man, one of them is of the fool. I am not of the fool, Mr. Holmes."

Holmes and I looked at one another, as though to share a collective sigh of relief. Men – especially wealthy older men – are often given over to flatteries and the disingenuous attentions of the delicate sex. Apparently, Despranos was not of that cast. His poignant remarks assured us that he was a fellow fully aware of the wily ambitions of his flatterer, and a man grounded in the authentic emotions of the ties that bind. He understood the difference between true family faith and the fawning ingratiation of an interloper.

Holmes explained to him that the family thought it best that the patriarch be transferred to a private hospital outside London. When the detective added his approval to the family plan, Despranos agreed without objection. With my assistance, the transferring papers were summarily processed, and a special hospital coach was engaged to accomplish the transport without delay. Holmes and I remained a few moments in the empty room after Despranos had been comfortably removed to begin his journey to his new facility.

Holmes stood beside the empty bed quietly pondering the details of some intrigue that I am sure was fomenting in his restless, calculating mind. "Watson," he said finally, "might I ask yet another favor? I do not want to overburden your official standing but is it possible to arrange for this room to remain unoccupied for a day.... perhaps two?"

"That should not present an administrative problem in the least," I replied. "Private rooms are not ordinarily in very high demand, but may I ask why, Holmes? Despranos will be safe at a remote location, and the Wrengle woman has no means of discovering the whereabouts of the new facility."

"Ah, you are a most dependable fellow, Watson. You have hit squarely upon two of my three thoughts in this matter: first, the patient is safe; second, the 'beautiful bird' cannot discover the new situs; and third and finally my friend, I am reasonably certain that Theresa Wrengle will return tomorrow or the day after at the very latest to visit her wealthy friend once again, and I want very much to have her find an empty room complete with a little parting gift from your old flat mate." Holmes spoke this slowly, and in a musing tone that seemed very pleased to have hit upon a plan appropriate to the circumstances.

The next day I was unexpectedly called to St. Gregory's to attend a colleague on a troublesome surgery. I fulfilled my obligations and was thankfully preparing to return home to an early supper. Visitors' hours had been over for some time. The matter concerning Senor Despranos had been put from my mind by the intervening duties of the day. I knew that he had been securely installed at a new and very capable private hospital, and as for Holmes's references to Wrengle's return, and a "parting gift," they were elements sufficiently insubstantial to remain but briefly in the thoughts of my otherwise fully occupied workday.

As I moved homeward through the lobby, a nurse from the geriatric ward called to me from the stairway. She asked if I would kindly accompany her to her ward, particularly to the room previously occupied by the relocated Spanish patriarch, Senor Despranos. She was not unsettled, but there was an undercurrent of anxiety about her request.

When we stepped into the room, the nurse pointed out a broken picture frame on the floor, and several crumpled sheets of bonded letter paper beside a large brown envelope lying on the clean coverlet of the hospital bed. Otherwise, the room was in perfect order. The nurse explained in a tone of voice both official and confused that staff had no idea what the frame and discarded pages were, and in fear that they might be part of some legal matter in view of the recent patient having so mysteriously left hospital "like a thief in the night," the papers and the picture frame had not been touched. I assured her that the items were without any significance to hospital operations, and on declaring that I would personally handle matters in an official capacity, I dismissed her to return to her regular ward duties.

When she had crossed the threshold to depart, I quietly closed the door and surveyed the room again. The scene was not difficult to deduce. Holmes's plan for Theresa Wrengle, the details of which he chose not to share with me the night before, had apparently struck its mark. As he anticipated, she must have returned to Despranos's room today to comfort the patient with yet another of her warm and supportive visits. When she found the room empty and his bed neatly made up, she must have realized that the patient had been discharged and had thus escaped from the poisonous circle of her influence. That much was clear to me. The broken picture frame and the scattered pages of a letter must be remnants of Holmes's "parting gift."

I lifted the fractured frame from the floor. It was a simple, inexpensive portrait frame with thin wooden edging. The enclosed photograph was a head and shoulders image of Sherlock Holmes holding his heavily blackened clay pipe and presenting to the viewer his ordinary mien of sober and resolute indifference. It was not a disagreeable photo, but clearly Holmes was cast in a somber contemplative mood. I cannot admit to Holmes being a particularly handsome fellow, but the photo did capture an arguably manly visage and one not to be immediately disregarded by the observations of the opposite sex.

I placed the picture frame on the bedside nightstand and turned my attention to the loose pages strewn on the bedspread. They were the sheets of a letter in Holmes's

127

unmistakable hand. The letter was marked with the present date, and the correspondence is reproduced below *verbatim*.

Dear Mrs. Wrengle:

If you are reading this correspondence, you have opened the large envelope placed conspicuously on the patient bed and upon which your name was prominently written. In addition to this note, the envelope contains a framed photograph of the signatory. It is offered as a memento from the gentleman responsible for bringing your unsavory marital activities to an abrupt end.

At the request of the Despranos family, I completed a thorough study of your movements, both about the Continent and in England. It appeared you actively pursued and entered into bonds of marriage with certain ill, elderly, wealthy, unmarried men. An explicit and detailed outline of these marriages, coupled with records certifying the particulars of each union, has been forwarded to my clients and to your erstwhile admirer, Giacomo Maria Santiago Despranos. Consequently, Senor Despranos the elder has been removed to a medical facility the location of which is to be held inviolate.

As a result of your attempt to enter into a self-serving marriage with their beloved patriarch, the Despranos family has committed all necessary resources to despoiling your future efforts to capture the affections of other unsuspecting gentlemen. As you are aware, the family's financial means are virtually inexhaustible. Accordingly, they will engage independent investigators to monitor your activities worldwide from the date of this correspondence to the close of your natural life. If their reports reflect actions similar to those in which you have been previously involved (eg. Williams, Meridan, Wrengle) a thorough and complete dossier of your past marital history will be delivered in-hand to the person of the gentleman, his extended family, and the local constabulary.

Yours sincerely,
SHERLOCK HOLMES

Several days had passed before I found myself climbing the stairs leading to the lodgings at Baker Street. I was anxious to hear any residual details that might have arisen in the wake of the Theresa Meridan-Wrengle incident at St. Gregory's. Being no surprise to me, the room was littered about with papers and the ordinary jetsam of Holmes's whirlwind style of bachelor living. The detective was shuffling through a blizzard of documents, looking for "...the blasted pages of my monograph for London City

College on the 'Duplicate Positioning of Carbon-Enriched Magnetic Plates.'"

"You see I have brought you back the broken photo and your discarded letter," I explained. "Perhaps you may want to catalogue them with some of your other case mementos... as reminders."

Holmes halted his search, turned to me, and looked at the pages and the frame I held out to offer him. "Thank you, Watson, but I think not," he remarked slowly. "With perhaps the solitary exception of your own bond, marriage is sufficient in itself to set the teeth of a confirmed bachelor on edge. A contrived and manipulated union is the ultimate incarnation of evil. There are some reminders, my friend, the conjuring thoughts of which deserve to remain unrecollected."

The Case of the Stableman

As a doctor of medicine and therefore someone whose training was concentrated heavily in the sciences, my views of the human situation run more closely to the practical rather than to the emotional or the dramatic. When faced with the difficulties of an illness or disease, a doctor's procedural path is a well-traveled one: A patient's complaints are heard, questions are asked, observations are made, physical checks are accomplished, and a diagnosis is rendered. The process is methodical and disinterested, and when scrupulously followed, there is a reasonable chance the difficulties of the illness will be relieved.

For my good friend, erstwhile roommate, and noted London detective, Sherlock Holmes, the human situation was hardly as neat and tidy as my science would have it. His view of our human nature was infinitely more complex than the superficial and rigid physiological models of medicine. For Holmes, humanity was a seething, tumultuous tide of motives, madness, deceit, and misrepresentation, and yet, in spite of the apparent darkness of his life vision, he was as carefree and Bohemian a spirit as any I have ever encountered. It is true that upon occasion, he could lapse into a vague and distant depression of mind and body, the release from which might span days or weeks of uninterrupted ennui. These bouts would wrack him unmercifully and unexpectedly. And to further complicate a thoroughly complicated man, he was never quite able to abandon his occasional use of narcotics. However, the use was intermittent and did not extinguish the bright lights of his sharpened intellect to any noticeable degree. Eventually, howsoever drawn towards those shadows, he would emerge, his thoughts pulled toward the crowded details of some diabolical crime or twisting international intrigue.

Mankind was a study for his analytical pleasures, and little more. In all the years of our long acquaintance I cannot remember any instance upon which he seriously considered himself in any regard to be part of the study himself. He is a good friend and a man of high moral character, but he is a detached soul – a car uncoupled from the limited express of his fellows.

I recall with misgiving my having intruded into one of his dark times. It was near Michaelmas Day this past year. The rain had been in a torrent three days running, the streets were rivulets from it, and downspouts and alleys hissed with streams of water rushing down from roofs and gables. When I looked up from the street, the windows of my old lodging were dark and foreboding. I stepped into the flat to see Holmes huddled in the armchair. The hearth was struggling to offer but a weak light and jealous hint of warmth. I tended to the fire and set it cheerily along before I deigned to disturb or even greet the restive figure of Holmes. His violin and bow were carelessly lying on the sideboard, and the air in the room was congested with residual smoke from the burning weed of his pipe. Taken all in, the scene was as depressed and deplorable an environment as it could ever be. The kindled firelight chased some of the drear, and so I called him gently, the third attempt of which roused him from his stupor. I was no stranger to these soiled episodes of his, so the sound of my voice did not distress or unsettle him. He muttered a greeting, pulled himself up into a sitting position, and did what he could to collect himself, although the effort did not produce any visible results. His lethargy had taken root. My clinical eye could tell he had not slept for days. I called down for tea and toast and sat with him some hours to assure myself that he was sufficiently well to pass the evening hours restfully. I knew that a letter in the morning post, or an article in The Times, or a message or messenger from some distracted sufferer, could throttle him back into the fierce vitality that was thoroughly himself. Until then, he would continue in his shadow world, no doubt pondering questions his crystalline intellect and startling powers of observation could not answer.

The rains continued, but Holmes's sun finally rose and he restored himself to the land of the living. When I returned on Wednesday, the evening of the day after my visit, he was alert, and conscientiously reviewing the pages of a large volume titled, Hardiman's Topographical Gazette: A Primer Review. I could not fathom how an 800-page volume could possibly refer to itself as "a primer review," but I kept the thought to myself and sat patiently until Holmes closed the imposing book and turned to face me. His recuperative power was no less a wonder than his intellectual. With the solitary exception of a voice left husky and rasped from the coating tars and nicotine of his overindulged tobacco use, he appeared to be in top physical condition.

"I see that you are feeling well today."

"Yes, thank you, Doctor. Was it you that visited me earlier?"

"It was early yesterday afternoon. You were somewhat indisposed, Holmes."

"I faintly recall having required some 'looking after.' There were toast crumbs in all the crevices of the armchair. I hope I was not too terribly troublesome."

"You were your inimitable self, Holmes. You are a blueprint whose lines I have become well acquainted with over the years, and may I say that some of the base lines on your print concern me. I will not bore you with a recapitulation of my Hippocratic oath, but I am duty bound to advise you – as I have so often – that your bouts of melancholia are debilitating things rather to be actively avoided than passively entertained."

"You are a scientist, my friend. You observe facts and draw conclusions, a process whose elemental parts we intrinsically share, but the conclusions drawn from your observations in this case are askew. My 'indispositions' as you call them, are not submissions to melancholy, but rather submersions into an alternative state of reflective consideration. They are not entirely the deep meditations of your Eastern mystics, yet they share similar features and seek similar results. I often find it necessary to consider questions, the answers to which, under the ordinary circumstances of conventional review, are not available. When that paucity of answers persists, unconventional methods are called for. Those methods are at the core of your medical apprehensions for me, Watson. Your anxiety over them, my friend, is a foundational stone in the edifice of our friendship."

"Intentional injury to the human body is injury, acquiring answers to questions notwithstanding."

"That is true my friend, but how many of our fellowmen down through the innumerable ages have sacrificed the banalities of personal health for achievement of results speaking to a higher order?"

"Yes, and how many of those sacrifices failed of their intent and left injury, illness, and death in their wake?"

"You exaggerate the risks, Doctor – an admirable yet hardly extraordinary predilection for you and your brothers of the physicians' tribe."

I was angling with all my powers of reason to formulate a reply that would dash the detective's argument to pieces, but my powers of logic had run their course, as they so often did when I crossed in debate with Holmes's incisive intellect. It is true that he was not an ordinary specimen of human health. His frame was long and sinewy and his level of muscular strength was well above the average. His vision and hearing were similarly at the outer edges of human capability, and I had known him to go without proper rest for days and not exhibit the least signs of languor or exhaustion. This present visit of mine gave convincing proof of his extraordinary vitality. In spite of several days of what might be referred to as severe clinical depression, he was as alert as anyone would have been had they enjoyed a perfect diet, proper exercise, and restful sleep patterns. My medical objections to his style of living were regularly disregarded, but I had to admit that after several days of a malaise that would have left most men physically distended, Holmes appeared almost buoyant. I had known him long enough to be certain that his exuberant mood must have its source in some new-found casework or other that had arisen to capture his imagination. It was only moments later that my prognostication was proven in spades. He rose from his chair and handed me a folded letter and its accompanying envelope.

"This note may interest you, Watson. It arrived with the morning post and contains some few promising elements that may be worthy of our review. In any event, it is an amusing collection of facts. The envelope presents an interesting story in itself. If you please, take a moment to review it and let me know what you think."

I looked with special attention at the postal envelope, hoping to discover the "interesting story" that Holmes referred to. It appeared ordinary in size, color, shape, postage, and inscription. It was beautifully hand-addressed to Holmes at the Baker Street flat, yet examine it as I might, I could find no extraordinary features to it, aside from a smudge on the sealing side, and a very small tear near the horizontal center of the piece. After completing my examination of this commonplace British postal container, I turned to Holmes, told him in detail what I had seen, and asked him what 'interesting story' the envelope had revealed to him.

He did not signal it in his demeanor, but I knew he was anxious to explain how certain minute elements of the paper contained probative data visible only to his discerning eyes. His explication, and what might have been a repetitive and exasperating spectacle for another, continued to be a source of fascination for me.

"The hand," he began, "is no doubt of the feminine cast, a fact verified of course, by the enclosure's signature. My study and subsequent monograph of several years ago reviewing 239 handwriting exemplars yielded many results beyond the relatively simple determination of the correspondent's sex. The length and angling of the letters, the proximate curvature of them in regard to their fellows, and the width of the ink flow from the light or heavy impress of the pen, mark this envelope as having been written by a woman in both a hurried and distressed state. The short-torn edge to the left of the postal address is not a clean cut as might have been made by the sharp edges encountered during the ordinary jostling of postal transit, but a tear denoting that the letter, after prepared for posting, was momentarily thought to be destroyed, then quickly decided against and posted nonetheless. This speaks to the note containing either a very delicate or very incriminating message. The smudge on the sealing side is the imprint made by the thumb of a man of large stature, rendered obvious by the famous maxim of Pythagoras 'Ex pede Herculem': from the foot alone – or the thumbprint – the man entire can be inferred. The content of the soil causing the thumb mark to be visible is organic in structure, most certainly common earth, although its darkened tincture denotes an agricultural sod that has been enriched by manure. The absence of a return postal address leaves the particular source of the note uncertain, but an agricultural province is clearly indicated."

Holmes placed the envelope on the lamp stand. I unfolded the enclosure, gave the paper a cursory review front and back, then turned my attention to the salutation and the words of the message itself. It read thus:

Dear Mr. Holmes:

I have your name from a neighbor privy to your investigations in Boscombe Valley. My son Thomas is a Master of the Oxford School of Engineering. He is recently home from an extensive business connection on the Continent, but his return was both unexpected and unsettling. London papers have covered a recent industrial theft in Austria in which I fear Tom may be embroiled, and from which I hope to extricate him discreetly. You are my only hope. Kindly allow me to speak with you on Wednesday evening at 7 at your flat. I pray the date and time are convenient.

Yours,

Regina Gottlieb.

I returned the letter to Holmes and glanced at my watch. It was half past six. "Aside from the literal import of the message, what have you been able to gather from the letter itself?"

"Very little aside from the obvious, I'm afraid. The correspondent is an Englishwoman, who married a German. The language and syntax of her writing and her foreign surname make that quite clear. Her son, highly educated in the physical-mechanical sciences, is presumably in the employ of Osterreichische Motor Kutsche, the Austrian horseless carriage company. The papers have been trumpeting this motor carriage business for the better part of a year. This Friday past, the Times claimed that OMK design patents have been stalled by failure to produce the final engineering calculations for the engine's precision valve train operation. The papers are presumed stolen. It is an unfortunate setback for what appears to be a promising enterprise."

"Really... a 'promising enterprise,' Holmes? I believe the entire matter is hogwash," I retorted warmly. "Horseless carriages indeed! They are nothing more than sluggish, noisome, unreliable playthings. The very idea of speedy travel and heavy commerce on London streets without the nobility and steady labor of the English equine is an absurdity."

"I share your love for the charm of the horse-drawn era, my friend, but the gasoline engine has struck the great bell of science, and it cannot be unrung. There may be strong reluctance, even resistance, but *bone fide* progress abides neither."

It was still well shy of the hour when the street bell was heard, and the light step of a woman's tread sounded upon the stairs. She entered the sitting room with a slight although visible unease, a partial reason for which was speedily forthcoming.

"I hope I am not inconveniently early," she said. "The rain is falling heavily without, and rather than hold the cabman, I thought you might excuse the intrusion of stepping in ahead of my appointment."

Holmes bowed slightly. "Your arrival is neither inconvenient nor an intrusion, Madame Gottlieb. I am Sherlock Holmes, and this is my confidential associate, Dr. John Watson. Please give me your coat, take a seat there by the hearth, and let the fire warm some of this wretched London weather out of you."

Mrs. Gottlieb was below the average in height, trim of figure, of an age appropriate for the mother of a young professional man and dressed in a manner that conspicuously put aside London's female fashion sense. A full cut woolen coat, long woolen scarf, shoes suitable for inclement weather, and a large broad-brimmed hat, proclaimed the sensible if not severe accouterments of an English *Contadina*. Many women in her style of dress, having found themselves standing in a somewhat formal English sitting room, might have felt the weight of sartorial impropriety. Mrs. Gottlieb was none of these. She appeared as comfortably self-possessed as she might have been in the hallways of her own home. Her smart and practical dress, however, did not shield her heart from its burden of care. She began to speak and almost immediately descended to tears and low spasmed gasps of breath, sure signals of a soul attempting to give voice to fears that have provoked and overtaken her. I quickly administered a small crystal of brandy and water which she gently put aside with the back of her hand and to which she could only whisper a barely audible, "No thank you."

Holmes leaned forward in his chair, and in the tone of voice he reserved for the sincerely troubled and harried among his intaking clients, said, "You have been brave and prudent to come here with your problem. Now speak of it and leave some of the trouble here in this room and we shall do what can be done to resolve it. You need not trouble yourself with the incidental data I have already gleaned. For example, that you are married to one Thomas Gottlieb who hails from the Heidelfrieden Province of Germany, you are engaged in the raising of excellent Dray horses in Nervinshire Downs near the southern borders of Scotland, you are decidedly opposed to all things modern or unconventional, and you had a heated exchange with your cabman this evening on your way to my flat."

"You have certainly done your research upon me, Mr. Holmes, but my husband's hometown, my aversion to modernity and my row with the cabman – though they ring quite true – how could you have ever learned of such things?"

"Aside from a vague reference to your son in the papers several years ago, I have done no research on you whatsoever, Mrs. Gottlieb, I assure you," said Holmes indifferently. "I suppose knowing 'such things,' as you call them, has earned for me my roof and hearth, room and board, although I do not 'learn' them – rather they present themselves to me almost unconsciously, it is more instinct than effort. Allow me to explain. When your celebrated son first took a berth in Austria several years ago, he was referred to in the London papers as Thomas, Jr., hence my knowing your husband's name. Your luxurious scarf, no doubt a gift from your husband, is woven from a very fine textured German wool blended in the Heidelfrieden Province of Germany, most probably the locus of his birth. The tenacious flecks of straw clinging to your rain shoes and the hem of your woolen coat are of the genus *Lolium Perenne*, a very

142

hearty rye grass species known for its high nutrient content and grown almost exclusively for the feeding of large dray horses in northern England. Your note to me was written in quill pen, a veritable antique for scripting in this modern age of metal nibs. As for your spat with the cabman, having arrived here 20 minutes early from the station was most certainly due to your thorough knowledge of the London streets. City cabmen, seeing a woman alone in provincial dress, would almost certainly attempt a circuitous route to a destination in hope to build a larger fare. Arriving early is proof that you corrected the gentleman's attempt to take unfair advantage, and 'put his nose to it.'"

The distracting amusement of Holmes's customary deductive acumen was a salve to the worried woman's agitation, and she smiled a moment in spite of herself and the burdens she carried.

"You are a keen observer, Mr. Holmes, and you see through to the core of things. God willing you can see a way through for my boy, Tom."

"Kindly tell us of the matter and include all possible detail. As you have seen, sometimes the very smallest of items can transform into important evidence."

"I fear I come to you without evidence of any kind save one – the disturbing premonition of a mother. As you concluded, my husband and I own and manage a large horse farm in Nevinshire. We raise dray horses for several of

London's heavy transport companies. Our son, Thomas, was not drawn to the family business. He was always a very bright boy and excelled at school in mathematics and science. As you are aware, he is chief engineer for an Austrian concern engaged in the design and production of the horseless carriage... or he was. After several years of commendable service, he left his post in great haste and without any formal notice to his employers. In my heart, I believe his departure was coerced by some third party, and to worsen matters, I feel as though the coercion involves me. The times of his hasty departure and of the theft of certain company papers correspond. Since coming home, he is a changed man, Mr. Holmes. He was always a steady and amiable fellow. Recently, however, he is terribly nervous and distracted, and so very solicitous of me that I know there is some darkness upon him."

Our conversant was so intent on her short narrative and we on listening to it, we took little notice of the heavy steps upon the stairs. When the page suddenly opened the door to the sitting room his eyes were wide with worry, and before he could announce the visitor, a young man burst into the room wearing a look containing equal parts of fear and anger. He was dressed in the current London fashion with perhaps a hint of the Continent about him. His coat was cut short, his boots somewhat square-toed, his bowler hat was trimmed with a wide linen ribbon, and his gloves were light gray in the French style of the day. Altogether, he was an inconspicuously modern young man about town. His gaze went quickly around the room until it settled finally upon

Mrs. Gottlieb. He turned in a flurry, pulled her coat from the rack by the door, and turned toward the hearth where she was seated.

"Mother," he said imperiously, "we are leaving."

Mrs. Gottlieb had been the very specimen of a self-possessed woman, but in the presence of this impetuous young man, she reverted to a gelatinous mass of silent compliance. She looked at her son worriedly, quickly lowered and averted her eyes from both Holmes and myself, then soundlessly and in one fluid movement, rose obediently and moved toward the young man at the doorway. As she reached for her coat, Holmes rose from his seat.

"If what your mother has just imparted to us, and if your present rather ungracious entrance is any indication of the state of mind you are in from your recently disengaged employment, I suggest you seat yourself and join us in delineating the circumstances of the matter at hand."

"It is a family matter, and none of your concern, sir," the son said abruptly, but his words had lost their heat. What Holmes had just spoken to the boy had hit a mark in him. His carriage softened, his shoulders relaxed, and the rigid stance that had but a moment ago looked threatening, now looked merely tired.

"It is of my 'concern.'" Holmes explained quietly. "Were I befuddled by some knotty mathematical calculation,

I would need come to you. When your matter is a criminal intrigue, you need come to me. It is a simple question of a proper division of labor, Thomas."

The young man stood by the doorway disarmed. He covered his face with his hands. The gesture pushed his hat back on his head and it fell to the floor. Mrs. Gottlieb lifted the bowler and gently placed it on the rack, as I retrieved the untouched crystal of brandy and water and urged it upon him. He stepped unsteadily into the room and slumped into the divan with the tumbler in hand.

"They have threatened my family, Mr. Holmes," he said in a flat and defeated monotone. "They claim they will begin by killing our horses."

Mrs. Gottlieb gasped at this. "No one would ever do such a thing! It is inconceivable! Who could ever harm an innocent, defenseless brute," she exclaimed incredulously.

"It has started already," her son added sadly to the mother, "though father and I have kept it from you. "Brutus, our retired stallion was found dead last month along the bank of Loch Everly in the Hempshire Paddock ." The young man turned slowly to face Holmes. "Father found the poor animal attacked and struggling and mercifully put him out of his misery. It is the Stablemen. They are behind the entire ordeal. I could tolerate financial ruin, Mr. Holmes, and being drummed from my profession, but they have said I must do their bidding, or my family and I will suffer a grisly price.

They have made their vaunting true with our stallion. I am entirely at their mercy, Mr. Holmes," he said in broken defeated voice, "but there is no mercy in them whatsoever."

"What do you know of your tormentors," Holmes asked.

"Their messages to me are signed, '*die Stallmeister*,...' The Stablemen. They consider themselves defenders of the international horse trade and oppose the horseless carriage as a mechanized abomination and 'a threat to humanity's peace of mind.'"

"Yes...yes," Holmes mused, "I have read about their emergence earlier in the century when the steam engine locomotive – the 'iron horse' – was their target for elimination. It is but small comfort to us that their efforts at that time failed miserably, for it appears we are faced today with a resurgent band of fanatics of that older stripe. The locomotive and the motor carriage are mere symptoms of their penchant for social disruption and aversion to progress. Their militant commitment against change is fueled by a righteousness that burns in the blind hope of creating a pure and simple world, a notion as naive as a spoiled child. They would have us all live in a sweeping pastoral landscape of gardens and fruit trees, but they would kill their own brothers to achieve it. They are a very dangerous lot."

The young man turned to Holmes and asked, "Do you agree to be my confidential agent, Mr. Holmes?" The detective nodded assuredly in the affirmative.

"Then I will admit to you, sir, that under the most dire commination to myself and my family, I have stolen all copies of the valve train calculations from my employers, the Osterreichische Motor Kutsche. The papers and calculations I have taken are all my own handiwork. Without them, the company's patent applications are utterly stalled, and without the patent grants, all production scheduling is irretrievably curtailed. I have abandoned my pledge and obligation to science, Mr. Holmes, and have become a criminal of the first order all in one fell swoop. My professional life is ruined, my family's lives are threatened by a band of ruthless madmen, and I see neither escape nor deliverance from any of it." He wrung his hands nervously and only barely kept his voice from revealing its emotion. "I am afraid I am thoroughly undone."

Holmes stepped over to the young Gottlieb and placed a steadying hand on his shoulder. "Only they are 'undone' who have been committed to the mold. There is certain hope here if the titular head of this radical organization can be discovered and his criminal coercion of you exposed. Doing so, however, will be no simple matter. This is indeed a desperate situation. Know that I will pursue remedy, yet keep in mind that 'desperate ills by desperate measures are relieved.' You have spoken of the 'messages' you received from 'die Stallmeister.' Are any of them available for my examination?"

"I have kept them all. They are locked in the desk of a small office I keep here in town for confidential OMK business matters. It is in the Roundsen Cross Building near Westerley Square market."

"Is your company aware of the office space you keep in London," Holmes asked anxiously.

"I am sure they are not," Tom replied. "The company prefers that all matters regarding the plans for the motor carriage remain undisclosed, even among its own principals."

"That is well," Holmes said relieved. "And the drawings with which you have left the concern, have you arranged for them to be held utterly secure and inviolate," Holmes queried again.

"Most certainly, Mr. Holmes. The company has been nothing if not an admirable employer. I would never consider compromising their interests were it not to protect the immediate well-being of my family."

Mother and son gathered themselves, and when all the customary declarations associated with departing clients had been accomplished, Holmes fell back into the armchair and placed the fingertips of his hands together, one of the characteristic poses he would strike when the various facts of a case called to him for their proper and logical arrangement. At these times, and certain others like them, he curiously took on the appearance of a player in a *tableau vivant*, with the notable exception that his purposes were not to entertain, but to think through grave and consequential thoughts. After perhaps 30 minutes in this staid, meditative state, he rose in a bound, handed me a sturdy letter opener, and asked if I could find my way to the young man's office in town, jimmy the lock of his desk, and secure the "Stablemen" messages. Had he handed me a loaded Webley and asked me to help him stand down a dangerous criminal, my response would have moderated not in the slightest.

"Yes I will," I replied, "if you think it will help the case along, most certainly I will."

"Austrian extradition is a cumbersome affair," he said offhandedly, "but I expect young Thomas will be arrested by the English authorities as early as tomorrow – the day after at the outside, so we need to make haste. He is an honest lad, and once in custody he will disclose the location of his London office and our chance to examine his little messages will be lost. We must strike tonight to be sure we gain the prize. While you are about it at his office, I will undertake some targeted research in the international arena. Thank God for the superiority of the British Library system, and for the confederate librarian or two with whom I have curried favor. When occasion calls, they can arrange for my 'special access' to the reference room stacks. Tell me, Doctor, do you have rounds at St. Gregory's tomorrow?"

"Not until early evening. My day is at your disposal. I can meet you here at the flat at 8:30 for breakfast if that is convenient."

"Let us make eight thirty the uttermost, and we will compare notes on this business. If my thoughts on the matter align as I think they ought to, we may yet retrieve this boy from the mold.

* * *

It was to be a late night for me, filled with the excitement that is generated by activities that are beyond "ordinary" and approach the edges of what may be referred to as "dangerous." Securing the messages from young Gottlieb's desk in the dead of night was not international espionage, but it did possess some of the intriguing elements of just such an undertaking. It was not the first time I had agreed to assist Holmes in an operation that positioned me at the outer limits of the law, but if what he asked of me seemed reasonably to suit the ends of justice, I could not in good conscience withhold my assistance. In any case, I succeeded in procuring the messages from the desk and did so without attracting the attention of either the police or the public at large. It was, all things considered, a very satisfactory evening.

It may well have been the excitement of my evening's intrigue, but when I arrived at Baker Street next morning, I was ravenous. Holmes could hardly prod a greeting and a few single syllable words from me until I had generously partaken of Mrs. Hudson's excellent breakfast provisions. It was not until I had begun work upon my third cup of coffee that my friend succeeded in wringing from me the most preliminary details of my nocturnal adventure. My report was nondescript: I had gained access to the office, opened the desk, and secured the messages the signatories of which were marked, *"die Stallmeister."* Holmes was delighted. He reached for the sheaf of papers I offered, repaired quickly to his desk, and examined the messages with his large glass as hungrily as I had descended upon my buttered toast and eggs.

It was the better part of an hour before Holmes resurfaced from his intense review of the notes which he intermittently cross-referenced against three folio-style volumes in German that he had apparently brought with him from his evening's visit to the London City Library. The books were large with heavy, thick brown leather bindings. From my glimpse of the gold-lettered titles on the splines and my very limited knowledge of the Hun language, they appeared to be police record books or accumulations of police files. The detective was still deep in this work when heavy steps were heard upon the stairs and in a moment the figure of Detective Inspector Lestrade of Scotland Yard was filling the space of the open door frame. Unlike Holmes, Lestrade was a man neither capable of nor concerned with keeping his thoughts and feelings in check. He wore both his head and his heart on his sleeve and his sleeve this morning proclaimed triumph.

"Begging your pardon for the intrusion, and good morning to you, Doctor – but I have stepped in to advise you, Mr. Holmes, that we have made custodial arrest of your client, Mr. Thomas Gottlieb."

"And the charge," Holmes asked without looking up from the desktop."

"Herr Gottlieb has been charged by Austrian authorities with the theft of industrial documents and international criminal flight. Extradition was processed this morning, and he was apprehended at the rooms he had taken at the Hotel Carlyle in Crosman Square. The young man mentioned that you were engaged upon his case. Without casting aspersions upon you, Mr. Holmes, this matter appears to be as "open and shut" as a copy of Blackstone's law. You might do well to think of your reputation and cut yourself loose from these kinds of foreign matters altogether," Lestrade opined, and planted himself sturdily in a posture that displayed a towering official confidence.

Holmes did not stray from the seat at his desk and remained intent upon the work spread on the desktop. His voice was measured and dispassionate. "Blackstone is a collection of commentaries, Inspector, it is not English law. As for the charges, you may be interested to know that Herr Gottlieb was sole author of the papers he is accused of 'stealing.' In the absence of explicit written and executed agreements with the employer, the documents were his to do with as his chose. Also, Austria is a 'free labor' nation. Consequently, leaving Austrian employment is not an actionable event. You may want to re-examine your extradition papers to confirm that they are more than 'evening wheezes.' Kindly forgive me now, but I really must return to my work of reviewing and evaluating genuine evidence."

Holmes's retort left Lestrade bereft of the ardor he had carried with him into the room.

"You must go about your business as you will, Mr. Holmes, and I will go about mine." The inspector mumbled his "good day" and ambled through the doorway and down the stairs to the street. When he had left, Holmes looked up from his labors, turned towards me, and gave voice – as he often did – to the shortcomings of those with whom he shared the burdens of criminal investigation.

"Lestrade is a good fellow, and a keen officer, but he is nonetheless afflicted by an infection pervasive in the officialdom of British criminal justice. When a connection in a case is discovered – any connection – it is seized upon and relied upon as though it were a dogmatic absolute. More often than not, such connections cannot withstand even the most superficial application of logic or reason. The discovered connection is then hastily coupled to other equally insubstantial connectors, and the theory of a case begins to spin utterly out of balance. Such is the inevitable course when a 'rush to judgment' prevails."

"And what is your present judgment of the case against young Gottlieb," I asked hopefully. "You have been poring over those messages and volumes with the utmost care. You must have arrived at some theory or some suspicion of culpability."

"A mother's premonitions, a son's anxiety, and the suspicions of Scotland Yard are our connectors here, Watson. We will add to these the written messages of a crazed band of zealots, a dead horse, one custodial arrest, an international enterprise on the verge of advance, and a national one threatened with decline. It is a fine kettle of fish. I have arranged by telegraph to speak with the local veterinarian who serves the farm country near Nervinshire Downs, and then with Thomas Gottlieb Sr., young Tom's father, at the family farm as well. It is a longish jaunt, but I suspect the journey to be worth the price of the roundabout tickets... that is, if you could spare the day from your duties. Your company would be most welcome, and if the matter falls out as I suspect it might, your presence may prove invaluable."

"You anticipate some danger then."

"Perhaps danger, but more likely desperation, and goodness knows those two are not strange bedfellows. In any event, some inquiries regarding these notes, the journey to Nervinshire, and a moments conversation with a few gentlemen of interest in the Northern farm district should put the matter squarely on the track.

*　　*　　*

It was a perfect day for a railway excursion through the English countryside. Low rolling hills and sweeping valleys' verdure were dotted about with barns and farmhouses, to make every window of the railcar a moving living landscape. Thin lines of roads and hedges and streams weaved through the green like ribbons marking out the fields and pastures. I suddenly recalled having once shared my wonder of this pastoral splendor with Holmes on a rail trip some years earlier. His remarks at the time were such as kept me silent upon this occasion. Besides, he was engrossed in a paperbound volume titled, Megerson's Aging of the Equine. I therefore left him to his studies and enjoyed the scenery without the benefit of his often-overcritical eye. At the station at Reversin, he ambled off to the local stationers and then to the office of Doctor Whinsee, BVMS, while I repaired to the local pub for refreshment and an early luncheon. When he returned somewhat earlier than I had expected, he explained that both the stationer and the veterinarian were remarkably organized and concise in their notations, qualities much admired by my fastidious friend.

"Notations upon what particular subjects," I asked.

"German writing paper, and the death of Brutus, of course," he remarked.

I will admit to being dumbstruck for a moment by the second portion of his remarks, until I recollected that "Brutus" was the name of the horse that had been killed by die Stallmeister to induce Thomas the Younger to his thievery. Holmes would not sit still for the simplest luncheon meal. He was electric with an energy that ordinarily foretold his having come to the conclusive elements of a case. He made hasty payment to the publican, and not a moment later, was hurrying us into a carriage bound for the Gottlieb farm.

It was a grand spread of countryside, with sweeping vistas, the beauties of which I am afraid were somewhat lost on the likes of two inveterate city dwellers. Thomas Gottlieb Sr., greeted us at the door of a large, two-story, yellow-stone dwelling house with an arrangement of tall thin windows and narrow copper shutters uniformly green-gilded with age. The homestead proclaimed a very prosperous family horse farm. We exchanged introductions and cursory greetings, and Tom's father ushered us into the study where no doubt the formalities of the farm's business were conducted. Gottlieb was of an average height, but very broad and very thickly built and gave the impression of a fellow who was immovably attached to the ground upon which his feet were planted at any given time. He moved in short deliberate strides with a slight swagger through the hips that must be the inevitable badge of the men who raise, ride, and train horses. In spite of the irregular circumstances of his son having been arrested and charged with serious crimes, he did not appear to be in any particular state of agitation. Rather, his somber equanimity was curiously disarming.

A broad mahogany desk was strewn with the papers, folders, and bulletins of his trade. He settled himself behind this formidable fixture and Holmes and I were seated comfortably in two high-back club chairs of the same rich red wood.

"My wife would have greeted you," our host explained, "but she is determined to remain in town to offer support to young Thomas... through all this business." When he mentioned his son's name, a very slight and very fleeting distress passed over his features. The look was so brief that I might well have only imagined having seen it, but I knew that if it had in fact crossed his face, Holmes certainly would not have missed it. "And I am afraid my apologies must go further still," he remarked. "I would have called up for tea to be laid, but I have dismissed the help... it is a day I had thought to quietly gather my thoughts and finish some unfinished work."

"Forgive me if I am being too bold," Holmes said decisively, "but I have come to inform you of the results of the investigations I have undertaken on behalf of your son Thomas, and those results cast serious aspersions of fault upon your person."

Strangely enough – and it was a very strange thing to observe – Gottlieb remained seated and silent, and appeared utterly nonresponsive to the detective's insinuating remark. The same blank, phlegmatic expression remained on his face. As a physician, I thought to myself that the absence of reaction to such incriminating words was either shock to an over-stimulated nervous system, or a fatalistic acceptance of an undeniable truth. In either case, it became apparent at this stage that we were dealing with an unbalanced individual.

"I have spoken to Dr. Whinsee, BVMS, earlier this afternoon," Holmes continued undeterred. "As the county's veterinary official, he is required to examine animals that are claimed to have been killed in conjunction with commission of crime or criminal trespass. He told me that your Brutus was an aging stallion. His days as a stud for mares had long passed and his health was declining. Of all the creatures on your farm, his natural death was imminent and his loss the least imposition to your business. If the farm had to lose a creature, he was most expendable. I believe you purposefully selected this aging creature, that you caused its death, and wanted blame to fall upon the foreign criminal gang, die Stallmeister. You told young Tom you found the beast suffering from wounds and put it out of its misery with a rifle shot. Dr. Whinsee has confided that, forensically speaking, the opposite is the true version of events. Your gunshot was the first and fatal application; the bodily wounds were inflicted *postmortem...* by you. The brute's death was neither an animal attack nor the heinous act of a fanatical trespasser, but rather the desperate action of a man whose darkened past had intruded into his present."

159

Gottlieb's eyes remained on Holmes impassively. His arms rested flat on the desktop and his hands were clasped together with the fingers intertwined.

"Your father's name was Thomas and your son is Thomas, but you were christened Heinrich Otto Vetterman. You were a spirited youth in the earlier part of the century – high spirited and zealously idealistic. Even at an early age, your dedication to die Stallmeister achieved for you a notorious celebrity. You assumed control of the organization, and under your leadership, its inveterate hatred for the technical progress of the steam locomotive became an international plague of sabotage and extortion. After several scrapes with German authorities, you fled to Britain and took your mother's surname to avoid connection with your criminal past. Your more recent history here at the farm reflects the very predictable path of the fanatic. Fiery youth descends into middle age, the righteous indignation of the zealot subsides, and the one-time radical awakens as though from a dream to realize the bounteous advantages of self-interest. Your farm achieved success, but your comrades of old came a-calling, did they not, Herr Vetterman? They knew that son Thomas was the spearhead of a developing industry that threatened the nostalgia of the halcyon days of horses and bridles and teamsters. You raised and sold dray horses – certainly you could be relied upon to fall in with them once again... and you agreed. The messages sent to Thomas were written by a confederate sent here to the farm by the Stablemen to make certain that you were following orders. He wrote the notes to Tom on German writing-paper stock,

160

which was an interesting diversion, except that he ordered the paper through a local stationer. You did precisely what die Stallmeister asked of you, Herr Vetterman, but you did not foresee the high price you would pay for indulging an old allegiance. You turned your son into a common thief, you burdened your wife with an insurmountable sorrow, and you exposed yourself as an international radical and fugitive from justice."

The German stableman remained seated at his desk, his heavily muscled forearms lying on the desktop and his hands joined as in prayer. He drew his elbows together and the crossed fingers of his hands came up to cradle his chin. He closed his eyes for a moment as though a resolution that had heretofore been considered, had now been resolved.

"You are a thorough fellow, Mr. Holmes," he said in a subdued monotone. "I admire thoroughness. You have struck upon my dilemma in each and every unfortunate detail. But tell me, my friend, have you the thought of any resolution to this troubled affair? No? Then I fear it is left entirely to the troublemaker to resolve the troubles as he may."

He said these words slowly and with an unsettling and chilling gravity. His next movements were unhurried, and he remained seated, but it seemed hardly a moment before his right hand was closed upon the grip end of a German Mauser pistol and he sat holding the barrel of the weapon to the side of his head just above and forward of his right ear. It is a fact

161

beyond our understanding that in the fractions of seconds prior to the exact moment of a calamitous or fatal event, time slows and the visual and audible cues to the human body become unavoidably precise. The scene was a slow revolving Mutoscope of images. Holmes was the first to move, and he sprang from the comfort of his chair across the desk toward the desperate man like a coiled spring. The flash from the muzzle lit up the wall behind the desk like a photographic bulb, and the sound of the shot in that relatively small room struck the ear like the charge of a cannon. Holmes, for all his adroitness, could not outdistance the pistol's fiery charge. It struck the mark, thrust the dense body of the farmer off his desk chair onto the floor, passed through the bones of the skull on each side, and lodged itself loosely in the plank of a wooden bookshelf. I rushed around the side of the desk to the crumpled form of the injured man, but my haste was for naught. The bullet had done its work. The slight pulsing of blood I could finally detect in the carotid artery, slowed, became more feeble, and ceased entirely in less than a minute. I cannot say that as soldier or doctor I am accustomed to death. Dying is not a thing to become accustomed to. However, I had never been in a room with a man who had conscientiously taken his own life before my very eyes.

Holmes was aghast but turned to me anxiously as I bent over the body. His expression asked me the result of my hurried examination, and when I shook my head in the negative, the "coiled spring" of only a moment ago was gone, and he slumped against the wall beside the desk and expelled a breath that seemed to deflate him entirely. He looked up at me with an expression that was difficult to read. It was not sadness and it was not guilt; it seemed closest to disappointment.

"I confronted him with facts the weight of which he was unable to bear, and he succumbed. I drove him to the edge, Watson," he said finally in a voice that was quiet, grave, and curiously unsettled.

"Holmes," I said gently, and repeated the salutation more than once until he finally turned his head and looked at me directly. "He chose a criminal's life," I said. "That choice placed him and his family in dire straits. You of all people know that crime has consequences. They may be deferred as they were here, but they hang above the criminal like the Sword of Damocles. He prepared for this day, his servants were dismissed, his mood was dark with the thoughts of what he had to do. He was a dead man before we stepped onto his porch."

*   *   *

In the weeks that passed after the episode at the Gottlieb farm, I stepped in uninvited at Baker Street several times to assure myself that Holmes was untroubled. These visits, purposeful as they were meant to be, were unnecessary, or so they certainly appeared. Holmes was engaged in two new matters, neither of which promised to seriously challenge him, but were sufficient nonetheless to divert his attention from one of the brooding moods into which I feared he might be drawn.

During the last of these impromptu visits, Holmes explained that he had prepared an extensive dossier for submission to Osterreichische Motor Kutsche in the hope it would restore Thomas Gottlieb Jr. to his abandoned post. It was complete, he explained, with his personal affidavit and certified copies of all supporting police documents. This magnanimous gesture on the part of Holmes proved to be as unnecessary as my surreptitious visits to check on the detective's equanimity. The young man in question later informed us that he had decided to spend at the very least the forthcoming year with his grieving mother at the family farm in Nevinshire. When we learned this, I casually mentioned to Holmes that his labors in completion of the dossier had essentially been for nothing.

"Dear Watson," he said sliding his hands into the side pockets of his dressing gown. "As Parmenides explained, 'there is no nothing that the word nothing does not name something.' Our young client lost a father under circumstances I would not wish upon a mortal enemy. My effort to restore his employment, as unnecessary as it may have been, is my Parmenidian 'something.'"

Upon hearing this exhortation and noting the suave and collected manner with which it was delivered, I was reasonably and gratefully assured that Holmes's balance was securely restored.

MX Publishing

We have been publishing Sherlock Holmes books since 2008 and have become the largest imprint of its kind in the world, with more than 600 titles and 150 authors writing fiction and non-fiction. As a social enterprise, MX Publishing has raised over $150,000 for good causes to date across the UK, USA and Africa. Our two founders, Steve and Sharon Emecz are mentors and advisors to several charitable organisations and in 2020, Steve was part of the World Food Program (WFP) team that was awarded the Nobel Peace Prize for works combating hunger.

You can find all our books on our website mxpublishing.com and through all major bookstores.

Our new books are featured here –
https://mxpublishing.com/pages/new-books